Joseph Woodfall Ebsworth

Cavalier Lyrics: 'for Church and Crown.'

Joseph Woodfall Ebsworth

Cavalier Lyrics: 'for Church and Crown.'

ISBN/EAN: 9783744779685

Printed in Europe, USA, Canada, Australia, Japan

Cover: Foto ©Andreas Hilbeck / pixelio.de

More available books at **www.hansebooks.com**

Cavalier Lyrics:

'FOR CHURCH AND CROWN.'

BY

J. W. EBSWORTH, M.A., F.S.A.,

AUTHOR OF " KARL'S LEGACY," ETC.

> For though out-number'd, overthrown,
> And by the fate of war run down,
> Their duty never was defeated,
> Nor from their oaths and faith retreated
> For Loyalty is still the same,
> Whether it win or lose the game;
>   True as the dial to the sun,
>   Although it be not shin'd upon."
>   —*Hudibras*, Part iii.   175.

LONDON AND HERTFORD:

Stephen Austin and Sons:

NOW FIRST IMPRINTED, FOR PRIVATE CIRCULATION.

1887.

The Issue of this Editio princeps *of* 'Cavalier Lyrics' *is strictly limited to One Hundred and Twenty-five copies for England, and Twenty-five for America (except a few special Presentation-copies for the Press, and private gifts). All printed on Dutch hand-made paper, unbound and uncut, rough edges. The One Hundred and Fifty copies are numbered and signed in MS., this copy being*

No. *70*   *Fbsworth.*

Molash Vicarage, by Ashford : Kent.

MESSRS. STEPHEN AUSTIN AND SONS,
PRINTERS: LONDON AND HERTFORD.

NOVEMBER, 1886.

Cavalier Lyrics.

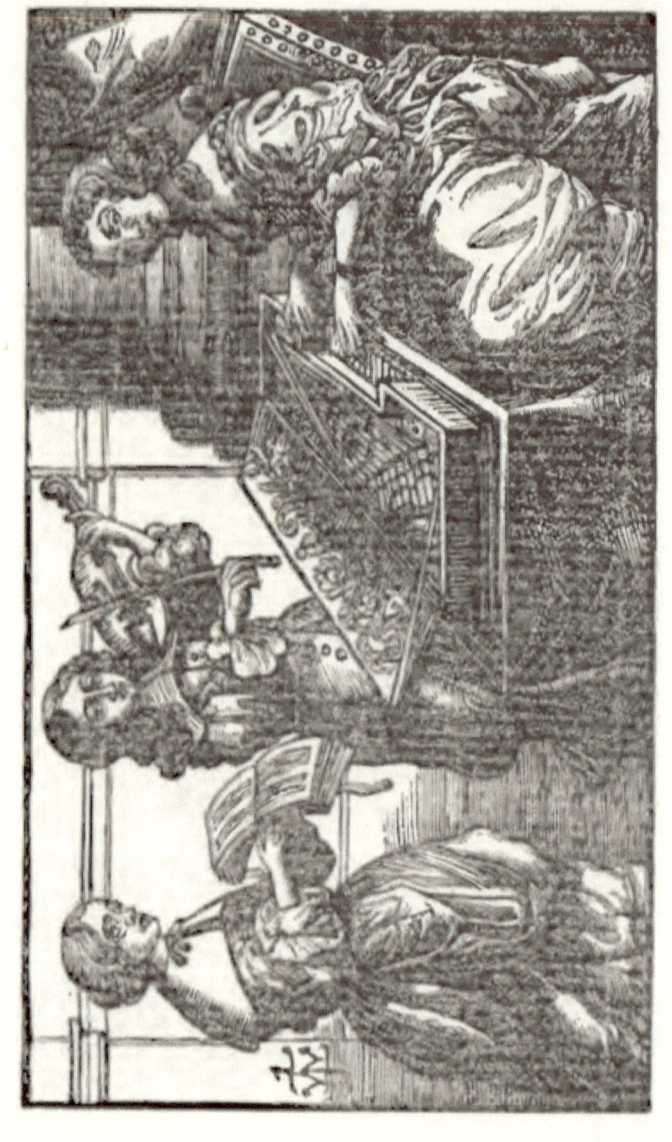

Frontispiece, by J. W. E., after one by William Vaughan in 'Musick's Handmaid,' 1678.

Cavalier Lyrics:

'FOR CHURCH AND CROWN.'

BY

J. W. EBSWORTH, M.A., F.S.A.,

AUTHOR OF "KARL'S LEGACY," ETC.

> " For though out-number'd, overthrown,
>   And by the fate of war run down,
>   Their duty never was defeated,
>   Nor from their oaths and faith retreated ;
>   For Loyalty is still the same,
>   Whether it win or lose the game ;
>   True as the dial to the sun,
>   Although it be not shin'd upon."
>   —*Hudibras*, Part iii. Canto ii. 17:.

LONDON AND HERTFORD:

Stephen Austin and Sons:

NOW FIRST IMPRINTED, FOR PRIVATE CIRCULATION.

———

1887.

HERTFORD:

PRINTED BY STEPHEN AUSTIN AND SONS.

TO HIS BEST FRIEND,

ONE WHO NEVER FAILED IN WEAL OR WOE,

IN WHOSE PURITY AND FAITH LINGERS THE SPIRIT

OF OUR CAVALIERS,

THEIR COURAGE, LOYALTY, AND DEVOTION,

J. H. L. De Haynes,

THESE

"CAVALIER LYRICS, 'FOR CHURCH AND CROWN,'"

ARE

DEDICATED.

1886.

TO J. H. L. DE VAYNES,

Of Updown, Thanet.

Friend, in whose sight these Lyrics had found grace,
More from thy generous kindness than their due,
Whate'er thy judgement deem harsh or untrue
   Gladly would I desire to here erase.
   Dead Beauties, my rough hand essay'd to trace,
Thy bright young eyes caught swiftlier to view,
With lessons that from early years we drew:
   The phantom glories of each haunted place.

Others may proffer better gifts than mine,
   More costly than such tribute I now bring
To lay in humble reverence at thy shrine:
   I know they cannot tempt thee hence to fling
One wreath thy servant's fingers loved to twine,
   Or hush the echoing lays he dared to sing.

                J. W. E.

" When as we lived in peace (God wot)
    A King would not content us,
  But we, forsooth ! must hire the Scot
    To all-be-Parliament us ;

" Then down went King and Bishops too,
    On goes the holy work
  Betwixt them and the Brethren blue
    T' advance the Crown and Kirk.

" But when that these had reign'd a time,
    Robb'd Kirk and sold the Crown,
  A more religious sort up climb,
    And crush the Jockies down."

           —*Marchamount Needham*, 1661.

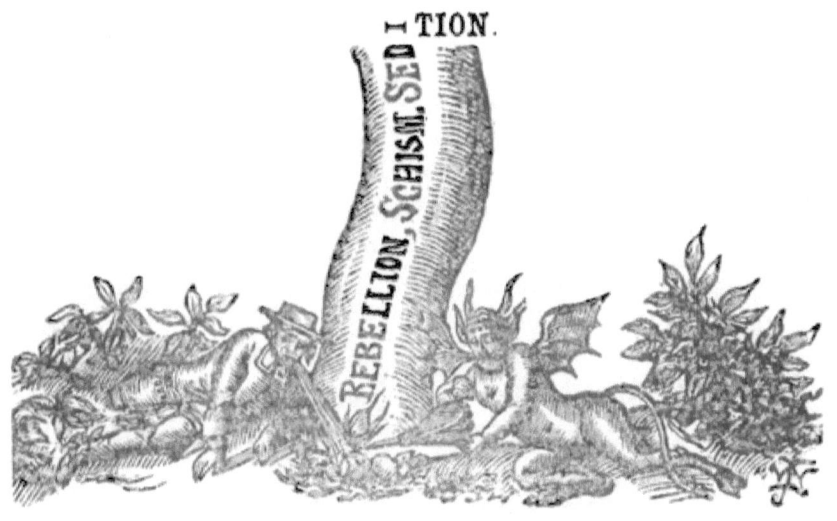

PREFACE.

" I stept aside to greet my friends."—W. S. Landor.

E ENTERTAIN AN UNEASY suspicion that a Preface may be regarded as a tyrannical infliction, and thus dissuade timid readers from marching any farther into the desolate regions beyond so forbidding a portal. But let them be reassured. It is a free country, and they are permitted now to 'take it as read,' without demur, as in another place. If they seek amusement for an idle hour, we tempt them not.

No elaborate defence of the political bias, avowed in our title of " Cavalier Lyrics," is needed by the few friends to whom this limited *Editio Princeps* is now proffered, in the Jubilee-year of our beloved Queen and Empress; close on the Bicentenary of the Revolution which over-threw James the Second. Undying is the interest of the struggle, in the middle of the seventeenth century, between prerogative of Monarchy and aggressive supremacy of Parliament; between an intolerant hierarchy and a still more intolerant assemblage of discordant schismatists, which came to a height in the Great Rebellion and Civil Wars: a struggle scarcely quieted at the Restoration. Overwhelmed by brute force, impoverished, exhausted, and almost disheartened, the Cavaliers remained true to their loyal principles, despite treachery and persecution. Only half fought, even in that long contest, the controversies remain to this day, ever fresh and alluring. Disputants repeat the old arguments, the old fallacies, the old errors, amid the altered conditions of our time, with similar injustice, similarly unsatisfactory compromises. Ever and anon the battle has to be fought anew. We ourselves have chosen our side, " For Church and Crown." Faithful to the cause we love, we can but fall with our face to the foe, like better men. But it is less a political than a social strife in which we engage.

In our days the popular writers, historical essayists and revolutionary declaimers, are accustomed to assail with blame every Royalist, ancient or modern, in order to exalt by contrast the regicides or the assailants of a national church. They claim for their republicans and rebels a monopoly of all the virtues, social, religious, and moral: individually and collectively. They refuse to acknowledge any faults in the anarchists, and hurl abuse against the loyal defenders of the throne. They strain out a Royalist gnat, and are willing to swallow a cavalcade of Parliamentary camels. Their loud declaration of intending to 'exercise generous impartiality,' to concede fair-play after patient investigation, is found to be a subterfuge, used unblushingly, to deal heavier blows against the Cavaliers ; who are always to be misrepresented, as necessarily in the wrong. Royalists are mere foils to the glowing patriots of the Commonwealth, who had at first so indignantly resented encroachments on their own liberty of speech or action, but who never failed to indulge themselves thereafter in licence and violence, whenever opportunity offered. Shakespeare instructively mentioned how "that in the captain is but a choleric word, which in the soldier were rank blasphemy ;" but these new-fangled Solons reverse the decision, and applaud the mutineer while spitefully cashiering the commanding officer. A Cavalier or a Tory must be suspected, denounced, and destroyed, at any cost. Whatever he does, or tries to do, is open to calumny. Mud enough being flung, some of it may stick.

Cavaliers had shown more practical wisdom in the true use of life than the Puritans, who made themselves and all around them miserable. Sour-visaged people, claiming to be the only true 'salt of the earth,' obtrusively denounced whatever failed to suit their own ill humour. They poisoned the well-springs of social intercourse. Their vicious intolerance blighted religion, art, and literature. They cast a gloom over earth. They did their utmost to misrepresent and unsanctify heaven. Life is full of beauty to the healthy-minded. When sorrow comes we bear it patiently, and recover strength, slowly or quickly, as the case may

be, without convulsing nature, or arrogantly blowing
trumpets in praise of our own heroism. Cavaliers do
not imagine that the world is weltering in sin, and doomed
to speedy destruction, simply because their tooth aches, or
a gnat may have stung them.

Surely we need more of the Cavalier spirit among us.
If we had it, we might then take life pleasantly, working
no less industriously, without being so noisy about our
religion or decrying other people's irreligion. Too much
commotion is made, far too much nonsense is talked, and
rabid salvationist rant encouraged, by those who ought
to know better. Let us avoid sanctimoniousness, as we
desire to avoid rebellion. The favourers of the one are
prone to the other. Mawworm and Anarchus generally
hunt in couples, as they did of old. Let us resist the
encroachments of Puritanical intolerance and ugliness,
physical or moral. Laugh to silence the re-assertors that
' Beauty is only skin-deep!' Who wishes to go deeper
than the surface, and burrow down into the skeleton?
Love a fair face, without disguise or shame; for the Platonic
doctrine is true, and a beautiful soul is generally found in
a beautiful casket. The mind fashions its receptacle in
harmony; although it has a hard task before it, after many
generations have been brutalized by a sordid Puritanism.
Let us love whatever deserves to be loved, and not insult
humanity by morbid discontent, vivisecting all that is fair,
all that is holy, in distrust and conventicle malevolence.
If life be made brighter to others, by sweetness and open-
heartedness, we cannot fail to share the happiness we so
readily extend. That is the Cavalier faith and practice.
It will be long before anybody finds a better.

The Puritan was always the most selfish of human

beings, yet he never learnt to understand or reverence the
true self within. To this day people prate about things
they do not understand, neglecting to cultivate the one
person who ought to be their best friend. A Cavalier
recognizes the value of being on good terms with his own
self; from whose companionship man cannot always
escape, be he ever so desirous of dissolving the bond of
union. Put this *alter ego* into good temper, by giving him,
when possible, the innocent pleasure that he loves best.
Do not unduly curb and bridle, or whip and spur him into
slavish torment (as the Puritans do); but let him have his
head occasionally, toss his mane and kick up his heels, so
that he may feel the turf under his feet and the free air in
his nostrils. In plain English (or in whatever inferior
language your Most Rev'rend Lordship of Bethl'am purlieus
prefers), let him read the books that he wishes to enjoy,
especially these "Cavalier Lyrics," and not only those
pretentious Manuals of Political Economy, Moral Essays,
Malthusian Warnings, Religious Disquietudes, Gehenna
Rediviva, Wellingtonia Puerilia, Protestant Safeguards of
Controversial Billingsgate, and voluminous Memoirs of
disagreeable people, who always kept eyes on the main
chance. Such books may be recommended and edited by
the illustrious obscure, but their opinion is not worth what
Chuzzlewit's Montague Fowler Tigg calls 'the ridiculously
small amount of eighteen-pence.'

The curse that fell upon our land during the growth
and prevalence of Puritanism needs the effort of every
loyal Cavalier to counteract it. More cheerful faith, and
less of arrogance in questioning Omnipotence; more holiness and less cant; more active fellowship and less wind-
bag oratory, or tyrannical interference with our neighbours'

landmarks, would soon restore the 'Merry England' that has almost faded into a dream.

In the ensuing " Lyrics," and poems scarcely Lyrical, are shown a few men and women belonging to the days of Stuart rule. While admitting that some of their opponents on the Commonwealth side may have been sincere in their convictions, resolute in courage, less stained with the vices of hypocrisy, rebellion and cruelty, than were the leaders who exercised a malign influence over them, our heart goes avowedly to those brave Cavaliers who fought and suffered unrewardedly in defence of the best interest of their country, willing martyrs in the cause of monarchy and religion : —

> Whom neither chains nor transportation,
> Proscription, sale, or confiscation,
> Nor all the desperate events
> Of former tried experiments,
> Nor wounds, could terrify, nor mangling,
> To leave off Loyalty, and dangling ;
> Nor death, with all his bones affright
> From vent'ring to maintain the right :
>> From staking life and fortune down
>> 'Gainst all together, for the Crown.

Thus had sang Samuel Butler, and we give some faint record of our loving admiration for him, and for his faithful friend William Longueville (to whose care we owe the preservation of the invaluable autograph manuscripts of ' Hudibras' and other poems). No less do our Lyrics show how dearly we prize the murdered Strafford, the impetuous Rupert, the revered author of the ' Religio Medici,' Sir Thomas Browne of Norwich, that noble divine Dr. Robert South, John Milton, with the diarists John Evelyn and Samuel Pepys. Also that sadly wasted *bon enfant*, Charles

the Second, whose best qualities are so constantly under-
stated, and his faults exaggerated, by the intolerant ignorance of our scribbling generation. Let "La Belle Stewart"
and "Nell Gwynne" plead for two, among the Beauties of
the Merry Monarch. We lift the curtain from "Our dear
little Village-on-Thames," one year after the Great Fire,
and show it also pictorially during the Great Frost of 1684;
even affording a peep at "Alsatia, after Nightfall." But
we have little space on our canvas for landscape, and con-
fine ourselves to ' Life Studies,' without fear of the ' British
Matron's ' prudery, hoarsely spoken at a Church Congress.

Most people now-a-days seem to forget that, although
there were swashbucklers and ' deboshed revellers ' among
them, the Cavaliers were true gentlemen, and that their
wives, sweethearts, and daughters were the noblest ladies
who ever breathed in England. How much *they* suffered,
what indignities they either cheerfully endured, or pined
under, until death released them from their persecutors,
it avails not here to tell. Perhaps our " Thirty-First of
January " (on p. 41), and " A Wayside Tale " (p. 50), may
speak for them. There must have been many such heroines
in those bitter days. Little does the present world know
what the women encountered, high-born and gently-
nurtured ladies, but despoiled, cast out to misery from
their heritage and home, amid that howling race of fiends
and hypocrites. It was fitting that the Cromwellians
who stabled their steeds in Cathedrals, and butchered
prisoners in cold blood, as they did the women after
Naseby, should have harassed to death the daughter of the
murdered Charles.

Elsewhere, and in a far more important historical work
on the Civil-Wars (concerning which see a *Note*, on p. 179,

of this volume), we hope to show much that is left here unrecorded: to mark that strange sweet sadness which fell upon Falkland, as a premonition of his approaching death; to behold Charles I. gazing from the tower on Chester Walls; or the brave Arthur Lord Capell, with his resolute bearing, mount the scaffold.

It is not without hesitation and prudent self-mistrust that any writer should permit his Preface to go forth. Whatever are the besetting weaknesses of each individual author, he stands exposed to merciless criticism so soon as his head and hands are beheld in that pillory, wherein he may be pelted safely with flowers of ridicule or drowned kittens of scurrility, by those 'Daniel come to judgement' who rejoice over their enemy being delivered bound to the Philistines, shorn of his strength, by having 'written a book.' Not that we, old offenders, are timid creatures and thin-skinned, or devoid of the wholesome tendency to enjoy a laugh, even at our own expense; as the true Cavaliers of former days were wont. But underneath the glittering mummer's robe of spangles, or the motley of the jester, we feel deeply the solemn grandeur of the subject here so lightly touched as our theme: the loyal devotion of the men and women who gave their fortunes and their heart's-blood generously, with all that makes life pleasant or endurable, for a cause that from the first they held to be just; yet for a king whose inherited faults of statecraft, vacillation and duplicity, were so incurable that his most faithful followers must have foreseen the failure of their efforts to replace him in power, even if they closed their mind against a conviction that he was unworthy of their homage and self-sacrifice. They were faithful unto the end, and their loyalty was its own reward.

Love is not love
That alters when it alteration finds,
Or bends with the remover to remove.

It is sad enough to remember the evil influence of Henrietta Maria; sad to make this confession of knowing it, later than two centuries after King Charles attempted his 'arrest of the Five Members' (a blunder, every way, but a small crime in comparison with the outrage of 'Pride's Purge' or Cromwell's forcible expulsion of the Rump Parliament, his armed troopers offering personal violence to the Speaker). How much more bitter must have been such a thought of old, to one like the noble Falkland on the very morning of the battle at Newbury which was to still the beatings of his heart and bring him 'peace'? If we failed to recall some of these Cavaliers to view, let not ungenerous ridicule be cast on them, because of our own inability to do justice to their deeds and motives.

With the exception of some half-dozen pieces (retrieved from the author's other books) all these Cavalier Lyrics are now printed for the first time.

[Since the publication of his two-volumed "Karl's Legacy" in 1868, the present writer has continued during the past ten years working quietly and not for hire on antiquarian, literary, and historical studies, for some of our book-printing Societies, such as the Ballad-Society, established in 1868 (editing for it the large collections of the British Museum, "The Bagford Ballads," "The Amanda Group," and the still uncompleted voluminous "Roxburghe Ballads," from the rare original broadsides: to these adding copious annotation and pictorial illustrations reproduced by his own engraving. *A few of these pictures are introduced in the present original work.* Also, earlier, he had edited three volumes of "Drolleries of the Restoration," such as are mentioned on pp. 70 and 94; also two fac-simile reprints of the "Midsummer Night's Dream" quartos (Fisher's and Roberts's) of 1600.

Thus for well nigh a score of years he has not offered anything
for general acceptance, and since he, in 1871, accepted an obscure little
Vicarage in Kent, his existence has been forgotten with his own un-
gruding consent.   He has been "lost to sight," but cannot flatter himself that he was "to memory dear."   Some of us are not ambitious of
being in vogue, like the authors of shilling dreadfuls or libels on the
aristocracy.   As much favour as was good for him was accorded to his
" Karl's Legacy " (long out of print) in 1868.   He can scarcely be
accused of pertinaciously obtruding himself on the attention of His
Stupendous Majesty the Public, even now when he steps forward with
a half-mocking smile, and lays his little volume on the door-step.]

There may possibly be a few willing listeners.   Who
knows ?   Such as they are, Lyrical and wise, or otherwise,
these rhymed records of Stuart days possess the merit of
sincerity.   Without attempting to defend either the statecraft or the sincerity of Charles I., any more than the con-
nubial fidelity or patriotic self-denial of his two sons who
successively ruled our unruly nation, it suffices if we have
honestly shown the portraiture of some faithful Cavaliers,
in war-time and in scarcely less troubled days of nominal
peace, believing that what we tell is the simple truth.
After all, the auditory to whom we appeal is composed of
friends who are the sole survivors of a goodly company,
fellow-students in art, science, and literature, from whom
we are separated but not estranged.

[Chief among these may we name the delineator of the depth and
beauty of Scottish peasant life, warm-hearted robust ' Tom Faed ' ; the
refined and genial W. Q. Orchardson ; the stalwart John Pettie ; the
bright cheery Peter Graham ; the earnest and poetic-minded John
MacWhirter ; the kind and unaffected ' Brothers Burr,' John and
Alexander : with that truest student of mystic lore and old-world
diablerie, Sir William Fettes Douglas, now President of the R.S.A.

Less widely dissevered from us have been the two several producers of "Poems by a Painter," both dear to us, and both from the North Countrie, William Bell Scott (surviving younger brother of our own early instructor, David Scott, R.S.A.), and Sir Noël Paton, Her most gracious Majesty's Limner for Scotland : noblest and purest of idealists and friends. There are others, no less certain to yield acceptance, and of closer intimacy : Arthur Henry Bullen, the accomplished editor of early dramatists, with ripe judgement and loving heart ; the venerable William Chappell, with whose studies we hold close alliance ; the true and untiring student, Dr. A. B. Grosart ; W. J. Linton, best of wood-engravers, yet separated from us by the Atlantic Ocean ; George Steinman-Steinman, F.S.A., of Sundridge, private biographer of many a Beauty who had graced the Court circle of our Second Charles ; James J. Cartwright (editor of Reresby) and James Gairdner (our most accurate and conscientious historian), both of the Record Office ; John C. Francis, publisher of the *Athenæum*, worthy son of a most worthy and beloved father ; James S. Mitchell, of Lower Clapton ; William R. Wilson and W. Y. Fletcher, F.S.A., esteemed friends at the British Museum (not forgetting the generous and learned Principal Librarian, Edward A. Bond, C.B., with the Keeper of the Printed Books, George Bullen, F.S.A., ever honoured both). To these add Matthew Arnold, whose "Scholar Gipsy" knows no rival in our affections ; our favourite nephew, William Walter Fenton of Melbourne ; Professor Thomas G. Bonney, B.D., with the Rev. brothers John and Joseph E. B. Mayor, of Cambridge ; Bertram Dobell (best of booksellers), of Haverstock-Hill ; W. M. Wood, of Hertford, King of Readers ; Dr. A. M. Adam of Boston : with James Muir Wood and James Richardson of Glasgow. The roll-call of our friends is not exhausted. We have not named any lady-friends, for whom nevertheless our volume enters into print. Chief of all is one to whom it is solely dedicated, and who (like the bright sylph, second in our list,) had seen every Lyric in earliest manuscript. The third remains unforgotten, and unceasingly dear, in either world.]

Many are the friends who have already passed away, in whose eyes this volume might have found favour for the writer's sake, and for the cause of the Cavaliers :—

Sie hören nicht die folgenden Gesänge,
Die Seelen, denen ich die ersten sang;
Zerstoben ist das freundliche Gedränge,
Verklungen ach! der erste Wiederklang.

Thus memory recalls, among those who might have greeted us anew, dearer than brothers, Henry Bradshaw and George R. Crotch, of Cambridge; William Brodie, the Scottish sculptor, and M. L. of Edinburgh; Thomas Aird of Dumfries, and George Gilfillan of Dundee; William Henry Murray of St. Andrews; the veteran Shakespearean critic, John Payne Collier; Harry Harridge, of Loughborough; and, above all, one whose honoured name the author bears, but whom he could never hope to equal, that Joseph Ebsworth, dramatist, musician, scholar and linguist, who lies buried in the Dean Cemetery of Edinburgh, at the feet of David Scott.

Let the book go forth, before other true friends have left the earth, and while the hand that wrote these Lyrics in honour of our Cavaliers is still able to add the little word—' Farewell.'

JOSEPH WOODFALL EBSWORTH.

MOLASH VICARAGE, BY ASHFORD, KENT,
NOVEMBER 10, 1886.

On the Coast of Ballad Land.

We went on a cruise to Ballad-Land,
  When the world was all before us,
We ran our light skiff on the shingly strand,
  And were hail'd with hearty chorus ;
There were sounds of wailing across the sea,
  Love-songs from the fisher-lasses :
The 'long-shore thieves shouted jollily,
  While they tippled and clink'd their glasses.

" Come hither, and dig in these mines for gold !"—
  " Come hither, and gather flowers !"—
" Come, hearken what grief made hearts turn cold !"—
  " Come, sport thro' the joyous hours !"
These, these were the voices we heard on the beach,
  With Siren invitations :
We yielded betimes, for we fain would reach
  The wealth of the Ballad-nations.

O! many a day in the years since then
  Have we sail'd with the same endeavour ;
And may help to pilot better men
  While we keep on our tack, for ever.
Sometimes we cast net in the treacherous wave
  (All is fish that our grapnel catches) :
Sometimes we drift shuddering over the grave
  Where the ghost of each Cavalier watches.

No Pirate we fear, no Buccaneer,
  Whose black-flag threatens mischief ;
We sharpen our cutlass, and raise a cheer,
  For we'll soon send to Davy Jones his chief :
Let Puritans snivel, let Prudes look glum,
  We laugh at their hatred of true-hearts :
With our 'Cavalier Lyrics,' old friends, we come
  To tell of our favourite Stuarts.

Placetne Vobis.

Happy are they, in Life's accidents,
Who reckon themselves among the 'Contents!'
Cavaliers, under unlucky star born,
Plunged into Pleasure's wide-open Horn,
Welcom'd and cheer'd by a social rout,
Till from thraldom they found no passage out ;
Then fools 'tee-hee'd' them, with wiseacre scorn,
But brought no release from the treacherous Horn :
Festivals none, but continuous Lents,
They spied through the grating : no more 'Contents.'

This was the pictured moral, in truth,
Two centuries old, of 'Extravagant Youth' ;
But we undismay'd make a new application,
Thus enriching the present Queen's-Jubilee nation :
Hoping glad readers may plunge inside
Our 'Cavalier Lyrics,' now open'd wide :
Where, contentedly lodged, they may ever reside.
('Neath a bushel we need not our rushlight hide.)

Non Placet.

(Vide woodcut of Molash, on p. 195.)

Harsh cynics, wandering through each garden fair,
Seek to find fungus growths, neglecting roses ;
So readers, counting nought here choice or rare,
May sniff disparagement at home-rais'd posies :
" Fie, what ill weeds are these! does the man dare
Commend them to our bosoms or our noses ?"
Grave Sirs ! in Hortus Siccus place we share :
Time tends Historical metempsychosis.

J.W.E.

CONTENTS.

PART FIRST—BEFORE THE RESTORATION.

PART SECOND—RESTORATION TO
REVOLUTION.

PART THIRD—MISCELLANEOUS.

Postscript-Preludes to 'Cavalier Lyrics.'

(Written after the others were printed.)

I.

My First Rondeau.

For Cavaliers and Ladies fair
An hour of leisure prithee spare
  To these my ' Lyrics,' though you take
  No interest for the writer's sake,
Not valuing mere pedlar's-ware.

Yet is he bold to here declare
They well deserve rhyme rich and rare,
  Such as poetic thirst might slake,
        For Cavaliers.

Smile you, or frown disdainful wear,
His page is humbly waiting there,
  Telling its tale of hearts that ache,
  Or throb with joy, or mutely break :
Then smile! all sullen scorn forbear,
        For Cavaliers!

22, xi. '86.

II.

How the Cavalier Secrets were Learnt.

Under my window I heard them crying,
  " Come away, Parson, we ghosts are friends!
Little you care about selling or buying,
  Whether society rots or mends.

" Long time you look'd back on us, who early
  Came to the world ere it lost its bloom :
Laugh at it still, be it sleek or surly :
  We never fear'd either dungeon or tomb.

" Oft we sat with you at midnight hour,
  Whispering secrets to you, as of old :
We, who have wither'd in London's Tower :
  We, who have slumber'd beneath the mould.

" Spectres of Cavalier martyrs ne'er daunted,
  One who well loved us, and loves us still :
Fairest of damsels your dreams have haunted
  Living or dead they your blood never chill.

Something we owed you, for faith unshrinking
  Something we paid you, by insight given :
You were not shock'd by our brawls or drinking
  Whatever our sins, we were duly shriven.

" Reckless of Self, we have never falter'd
  When we were summon'd for Church or Crown
Laugh'd at our foes, not like recreants palter'd
  Duty commanded, we laid life down

" Flung it away, somewhat rashly, and wasted,
   Better than grudgingly counting the cost :
Thus only highest delights are tasted ;
   Thus only saved is the life we lost.

" Parson ! you care not who rails or blesses,
   Choose your own friends from our ranks thrice-told ;
Spectres can yield you their best caresses :
   Ours are the love-gifts that never wax old."

22. xi. '86.

III.

My First Rondel.

Poor little Lyrics ! who now shall greet you :
   What vacant place is in cage or bower ?
   Shelter is none beside fount or flower ;
Never a maiden will hasten to meet you.

Harsh-tongued Critics with rod may beat you,
   Pick out your faults in a bad half-hour ;
Editors, centuries hence, complete you !
   What vacant place is in cage or bower ?

Who in their heart shall enthroning seat you :
   Flatter you, owning your spells have power ;
   Counting you wealth, though of scanty dower ?
Shall there be none to cry, " O ! you sweet, you !"—
Poor little Lyrics ! who now shall greet you :

22, xi. '86.

IV.

En Our Old-English Home.

(Greywell-Hill, Hants, August, 1669.)

" *Come, tell us a tale of the Wars, Uncle Joe,*
To please little Winnie and me ;
For the Chase is all sodden'd with half-melted snow,
And the fog settles down on the lea.
We can sit round the fire, as quiet as mice,
Or talk whatsoever we please ;
To hear about Naseby and Rupert is nice :
Although Winnie the kitten will tease.

" *I want to know who made that cut on your brow,*
And whether you kill'd many men ?——
Are there never to be any more battles now,
So that I may kill some ?—tell me, when ?
I am tired of books, that are stupid and dull,
Or of being kept mum, day by day :
I should like to go soldiering, slashing a skull,
And to keep shooting Cromwells for play.

" *Tho' now but a white streak, yet O ! what a gash*
It must surely at first blood have been !
Did you look very handsome in helmet and sash,
When you help'd out of England the Queen ?
Cousin Ralph does not like her, 'that Papist !' he says ;
But I know you were loyal and true :
And if you sing ' Lyrics,' while Mirabel plays,
I will be the best listener to you."

25, xi. '86.

⋯⋯

Postscript Table of First Lines.

Cavalier Lyrics.

PART I.—BEFORE THE RESTORATION.

Who enters this quaint Hostelrie need bring
No peevish visage and no railing tongue,
Grudging if merry Lays betimes are sung,
*   Hating to hear the clinking glasses ring:*
Our choicest viands on the board we fling,
Ripe fruit with dewy flowerets group'd among,
Such as Iacchus loved when Earth was young—
*   Autumnal grapes, and garlands of the Spring.*

Come! though at times satiric notes may sound,
*   Fear not lest words unfitting meet your ear;*
Fair modest maids and lovers gather round,
*   We show you Worthies of each bygone year,*
Scholars mature, warriors, and sage profound:
*   Leave prejudice behind! it mars the cheer.*

Prelude.

A Cavalier's Bower.

Is it not well, in a Quiet Nook,
    Such as our Priory here in Kent,
To toy with a flower, a print, or a book,
    Till the winter months be spent ?—

Not enough of the Flower for a botanist,
    Or enough of the Print for an amateur ;
So much of the Book that a moment miss'd
    From its page is a loss past cure.

Let snow, if it please, enclose me round,
    And the hurricane scatter boughs of trees ;
I shall fret not, or chafe, while tempest-bound,
    In a house with joys like these.

Blow hence, wild wind ! the peevish fools
    Who grumble at Cavaliers' harmless mirth ;
Who would chain up others in rusty rules,
    And make a big Jail of Earth.

Let them wrangle, far hence, while here I stay,
    With books heap'd round me, when trees are bare;
These leaves will not wither for many a day:
    Though flowers fade, little I care!

Each day is needed for some fresh draught
    From the fountains and wells of earlier time;
Whereout, since my own first years, I quaff'd
    The cooling waters of Rhyme.

Time was, when I liv'd in a Lady's eye,
    Her frown brought my sorrow—her smile, my laugh;
She had power to make me grovel or fly:
    My case now is better by half.

I can summon to love me fair Helen of Greece,
    I can listen to Sappho's sweetest lays;
All the brightest dames of old histories
    Encircle me, nights and days.

Every scene that I view'd when my heart was young,
    While the world I trod, light of heels and purse,
Comes back again, with each foreign tongue,
    Singing 'Welcome!' in dainty verse.

I won a free-pass to Elysian Fields,
    Where sickness and sorrow never intrude;
A Bookman's privilege always shields
    From whatever blast blows rude.

I ask no fame for myself, but give
   All praise to the bards who bloom'd and died ;
I seek no joy save with them to live
   In the Shadow-land, side by side.

They welcome me there, for my love unfeign'd,
   True homage to them I gladly pay ;
To read their souls is a joy unpain'd
   By suspicion of foul play.

Seldom abroad do I care to look,
   At the glittering crowds in Mall or mart ;
Since I find content in my Quiet Nook,
   And dwell, like a star, apart.

CHALLOCK-LEAS, KENT,
   October 10th, 1874.

A Child's World.

Far, far away from the noise and strife
That silly mortals mistake for life,
Dwelling securely in faith and love,
With beauty around, within, and above,
Thy heart attuned to each sound of bliss
That the gods bestow on a world like this,
(Which is either, to scornful or thankful eyes,
A Gehenna of woe or a Paradise,)
Thou, little maiden, I fondly pray,
Shalt flourish and smile for many a day:
   No cares to dim thy bonny blue eye,
   Save the broken toys of Infancy.

Darling wee maid, from the dim Unknown,
How is it thou seemest my friend, my own?
How is it thy form so often gleams
With a thrill of delight in my waking dreams,
And thy baby prattle sounds in my ears,
Till I turn aside from the whisper'd fears
Of a nature too prone to be gloomy and sad,
With thee to rejoice, again hopeful and glad?

I know that God sent thee to brighten earth,
With thy tender bloom and thy innocent mirth,
To speak unto us, who are old and worn,
Of eternal youth, with the soul new-born :
  For the gates of Heaven are opened wide
  To the childlike faith, but are closed to pride.

Come, yet again ! sit here amid flowers,
And linger awhile in the sunlit hours ;
Mingle with all that is new and fair,
With all that is wondrous and choicely rare.
Ask me to tell, what I scarcely know,
Unfolding the marvels the seasons show .
The tiny insects in glittering mail,
The modest flowers, the clouds that sail
Above the lark, as he pours his song
With exultant joy to entrance thee long.
Of the trickling brook, by the fronds of fern,
The moss and the lilies, thou fain would'st learn,
Whence it hath come, and whither it goes,
From springs in the earth to the river that flows
Onward in majesty far far away,
Till it joins the ocean where dolphins play,
  Around ships that wander to distant land :
  I see thee listen, and understand.

All things are 'waiting thee : joyfully range
Through the world that is opening new and strange ;

Watch the stars come, now faint, now bright,
When the twilight fades into Summer night;
Ponder each changeful phase of the moon,
List to the buzz of the bee at noon,
The hum of the gnat, the hedge-crickets' chirr,
The blackbird's whistle, the pheasant's whirr,
The solemn lowe of the cattle at eve,
The stock-dove's complaint, that seems to grieve
  In the deep still wood, when all else is hush'd,
  And we pity the worm that our foot has crush'd.

I would have thee grow, with thy warm young heart,
To feel that thou art not from these apart,
But loving whatever thy Maker placed here,
Walk on, firm in faith, without doubt or fear;
Reading with humble yet watchful gaze
The works He has shown for thy joy and praise,
  And striving, with prayer that His aid may bless,
  To yield all around thee happiness.

Darling, my darling! well do I see
Thou teachest us more than we can teach thee,
For the dream of thee, in thy faëry grace,
Thy silvery voice and thy rosy face,
Have told me sweet tales that I know are true
Of the holier earth thou livest to view:
  And I fain would speak unto others the truth
  That I learnt from a maiden's earliest youth.

For she came fresh from heaven, short time ago,
And heard not the evil whispers that flow
Stealthily, foully, on poisonous breath,
From those who make earth like the shores of Death ;
Men who despair of a future bliss
To atone for life's failure and agonies.
Thus she came like the light, the dawn of day,
To cheer us anew on our dreary way :
    Happy the lessons that have beguil'd
    From gloom, at the spell of a laughing child.

MARKET-WEIGHTON, YORKSHIRE,
    July 8th, 1865.

The Puritans of Old.

(Answer to the Epitaph, at Lydd, on John Mottesfont, Vicar, 1420.)

[PREFATORY NOTE.—A memorial brass at Lydd in Kent preserves the Epitaph of John Mottesfont, Vicar, 1420, a Puritan ante-Puritani :—

> Qui tumulos cernis, cur non mortalia spernis ;
> Tali namque domo clauditur omnis homo ?
> Regia majestas, omni terrena potestas,
> Transiet absque mora, mortis cum venerit hora,
> Ecce corona datur nulli, nisi rite sequatur
> Vitam justorum, fugiens exempla malorum,
> O, quam ditantur qui cœlica regna lucrantur !
> Vivent jocundi, confessi crimina mundi.

Such was the original Lydd epitaph, of which a translation in rhymed verse, by E. T. B., Lydd, appeared in 1845 (probably by E. T. Bass),

"Do thou the tombs beholding here, count the world's pleasure nought,
  To such a dwelling-place as mine shall ev'ry man be brought," etc.]

AUDI ALTERAM PARTEM.

O Mortal man, who years ago laid down to take thy rest,
Leaving thy mournful Epitaph for us, a grim bequest,
We know, as well as thou could'st know, these truths—that
    men must die ;
That all the brightest forms must fade ; that Pomp is vanity :
But we have learnt to smile at brows that always wear a frown,
We prize a Hermit cowl no more than tinsel Pageant's
    crown.

Sententious wisdom dooms our joy, 'because it quickly
    ends?'—
As well declare, because some die, 'tis folly to make friends.
'Our flowers must fade, ere winter snow falls from the
    gloomy sky?'—
These flowers we more gladly prize, before their beauties die.
'Youth flits away on hasty wings?'—then quickly catch
    the bloom,
And keep its memory in our heart, until we reach the tomb.

O grim sick-hearted Puritans! who long this earth have trod,
Ye are unworthy of the flowers, the sunshine, gifts of God.
It is too much to darken Life, with your cold threats and
    fears;
It is too much to veil the Heavens, with thunder-clouds
    and tears.
Our warmer hearts you shall not chill, our cheerful faith
    not dim;
We see a bright new world uprise, beyond th' horizon's rim;
Too long in gloomy sepulchres the springs of Joy lay hid:
Sons of the Morning, soar with us, above the Tombs of Lydd.

THE PRIORY, MOLASH, KENT.
October 10th, 1880.

The Ballad of Olden-Time.

(Before the Civil-Wars began, 1636.)

Only one little song!
With a few chords from her Lute,
Stop the pulse of your heart so strong,
Make the clamours of Folly and Wrong
  In an instant be hush'd and mute:
    For the days of old,
    The Beauties now cold,
Live again in that ballad sung:
The world shines bright and young.

Say not the Past is dead,
  That our world forgetteth theirs:
As though Love were for ever fled,
Or their tears had been vainly shed,
  Since we yield unto sordid cares:
    For each warrior true
    Whom of old they knew
Has left us example bright,
To struggle and die for the Right

Sir John Suckling's Troop of Horse.

(*May and June*, 1639.)

I.—HOW THEY STARTED NORTHWARD.

" Gallantly, jauntily, speed we all on,
Proud of ourselves and our leader Sir John :
Never a handsomer better-drest crew
Set out for loyal fair Ladies to view.
Brightly the sun shines, like silver our swords,
Dainty cravat with lace-ruffles accords ;
Gauntlet all stainless, neat-fitting, well suits
Sky-raking beaver and earth-scorning boots,
Red-heel'd, toe-pointed, embroider'd and gilt :
We shall be welcome when blood we have spilt.
White are our doublets, gay scarlet silk lines ;
Broad belt with buckle our slim waist confines ;
Hat, plume, and loose coat, all bright, cherry-hued ;
We are ' the Roaring-Boys,' never subdued.
Mounted on horses, high-prancers and fleet,
Brave Suckletonians, one hundred complete :
Who all together for King's use are got,
So tremble old Lashley, thou pestilent Scot !
When we come nigh thee, thou'rt sure to turn tail ;
Such a bright company never can fail :
Rings on our fingers, and spurs upon heel,
Woe to the foes who encounter our steel.
  Gallantly, jauntily, speeding well on,
  Proud of ourselves, and our leader, Sir John."

II.—How they approached Dunse.

" Halt we a day on this pleasant greensward,
   Need we set pickets to keep watch and ward?
   Gracious! three splashes on cloak from the mire;
   Stitches have dropt, here's a rent from some briar!
   How the new saddles have tarnish'd our hose;
   Gauntlets will tight be, when dealing out blows.
   Weather looks changeful, and much we shall fret
   Should roads be rough and a soaking we get.
   Had we but known such discomforts might be,
   Better to rest in our homesteads were we!
   Well, since our duty commands us to serve,
   Let us refresh ourselves, keep up our nerve.
   Tap a fresh barrel there! silver cups all,
   Brought with our mails complete by henchmen tall.
   Scarce half our dainties we get when we dine;
   'Drink we tobacco,' if short comes our wine.
   Pest on it, gentlemen! why need we haste?
   Life is not worth a groat, squander'd in waste.
   Arúndell knows how the campaign to plan:
   Sound then the bugle as late as you can.
   What, boot and saddle so soon! are you sure?
   Such inconveniences warriors endure!
   Help me, Tom, tighten his girth, slack his rein!
   Now we are mounted, and trot off again:
       Gallantly, jauntily, speed we all on,
       Proud of ourselves, and our leader, Sir John."

III.—When they omitted to vanquish Lesley.

" Hurriedly, flurriedly, out and alack !
 Ten thousand devils to hasten us back !
 Hey, helter-skelter, quick, out of the way !
 Who ever saw so disastrous a day ?
 Leave we our baggage, our colours, and drum ;
 O ! what a pickle if Lashley does come.
 Savages, cannibals, ill-bred, unclad ;
 Worse than wild beasts they are, raging, half mad !
 Sooner I'd meet a wild cat in a wood,
 Than such a pack of Scots, thirsty for blood.
 What were we thinking of, risking our bones
 Over this North-road, all bristling with stones ?
 What was the use of our riding so far ?
 We might have waited till South came the war.
 Why did we gayest apparel put on,
 Summoned by glory and little Sir John,
 If we were fated to lose here our health,
 (Suckling confessedly wasted his wealth),
 Tramping up Cheviot hills, fording of streams,
 Hearing such yells, and uncouth noisy screams ?
 Such a vile pack as this Lashley brings on,
 To discomfit the horsemen of dainty Sir John !
 Hark ! they come nearer ! we're fools if we stay,
 When savage caterans howl thus by day.
   Hasten, brave comrades, O hasten we fast !
   If we await them, this moment's our last.

Gallop then, gallop, and gallop right on,
'To the devil leave th' hindmost and little Sir John!
Dig in your rowels, don't spare the steed's bowels,
Flee from the Kelts who have no use for vowels:
Spluttering, stuttering, Gaelic or Erse,
Yelling unmusical Scotch forms of curse:
They love no Englishman, only his purse.
  If they once catch hold of cloak, it is gone!
  Then, pray, whoever can face our Sir John?"

Strafford.

(*Tower-Hill, May* 12, 1641.)

Not thine the lot to waste with grief,
  To sicken with a failing heart;
Rotting like sodden'd autumn leaf,
  When all Life's kindly buds depart.

Not thine to linger, a late guest,
  When mirth and fellowship have sped:
True Pilgrim, now hold on thy quest
  Before the twilight hour hath fled.

"Put not thy trust in princes!" Thou
  Avenged by that one word dost die:
Victim, yet victor, dauntless brow
  Can thy worst murderers' hate defie.

While they were Young.

(Boston, Lincolnshire, February 14, 1640.)

Comes a voice at early morn
  To the ear of Ladie-mine,
  When the sun begins to shine,
Sounding plaintively, forlorn :
      " Valentine !
Dear Maid Marion, do not scorn !
  Be my Valentine ! "

Laughs the bonny bright-eyed girl,
  Far too young to frown or pine ;
  While some ribbon gay they twine,
To repress each truant curl.
      " Valentine ? "—
Chides the Nurse : " Some idle churl !
  Not true Valentine."

Time will come for lovers' moan :
  If we read aright the sign,
  Factions round us now combine,
Threatening danger to the throne.
      " Valentine ! "
Loyal Cavalier she'll own,
  For her Valentine.

C

What my Cavalier sang, last Summer.

(Psyche at Lannercourt Grange, June 25, 1641.)

"Lady, my Lady, if hearts are in tune,
  Surely you hear the sweet music of June?
  Sunshine and roses and coverts of shade,
  Languor and rest, for young lovers are made.
  Droopingly bends yonder noble ash tree,
  Forming a shelter for you, love, and me.
  Here can we welcome the fresh breeze of morn,
  Scented with bean-flower, rustling the corn;
  See in the distance the village lie quiet,
  Far enough keep the town's worry and riot;
  Sheep resting near us, in patches of shadow,
  Such as they love, under elms in the meadow.
  No one to summon us hence to a task,
  No one to hasten, or question to ask.
  Need you not weary those fingers, or fret,
  Birds give us music without your spinet:
  Bees buzz around us in joy from the flowers,
  All things feel happiness: why not take ours?
    'Now, love, or never!' they say, 'for too soon
    Youth flits away with the roses of June.'"

When the Parliament had shown its Teeth.

(Oxford, July 15, 1642.)

" You may argue and rave, but little I care
    For the frothy rant of the Parliament crew.
  There were woes to redress, and wrongs to repair,
    Good work to be done, had their men been true ;
  But they came up in malice and spite and pride,
    Mischief they wrought against Church and State,
  To pass wholesome laws they scarcely tried,
    For vengeance they thirsted, and would not wait.

" Granted, things had not gone smoothly or well,
    Those pestilent Scots had stirr'd our blood ;
  But when sectaries doom'd Laud's soul to hell,
    And Strafford to death, could that turn to good ?
  If our own Cavaliers had only foreseen
    Where the crowd of rebels were driving us on,
  They had earlier rallied in strength, I ween,
    Not tried to bolt door when the steed was gone.

" Wise for the future I hope we shall be,
 If we ever make head, and regain the lost ;
We'll beware of helping the enemy
 By our wavering votes : we count the cost.
Palter not, Loyalists, then with your trust,
 Give up no outpost, retreat no foot,
But fight, till your arms be hack'd off, for the Just,
 And defeat cannot shame us, or death to boot.

" Words ? they are idle ! the time is come
 When deeds must approve which side we choose.
Demagogues shout, but we beat the drum ;
 Rebellion invites us, in scorn we refuse.
Sharply we pierce through their specious pleas
 Of ' freedom and conscience and commonweal ; '
' The People sole Power '—such tyrants as these !
 We answer no longer with words, but steel."

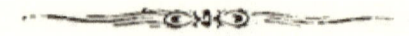

The Royal Standard raised at Nottingham.

(*August* 25, 1642.)

" It seems hard at the end to have nothing to show !
Could you pay me, Myrtilla, the debt that you owe
For the years I have wasted in longing and woe ;
For the weariness, anger, and envy I felt,
When you smiled on some rival of mine, who had knelt
At your feet in Fool's Paradise, where I had dwelt :
    Were you kind now an hour for each year from me shaken,
    I were happy one day, and you never forsaken.

" Say, confess, if among all my rivals you found
One who match'd me in love that was honest and sound,
While you kept us like butterflies fluttering round ?
Was there one who could so prize your beauty as I,
Whom you scarce gave a smile to, or droop of your eye,
As a modest reward for my lingering nigh ?
    You held my heart captive, your measures were taken
    To yield me no guerdon, yet not be forsaken.

" Now the Standard is rais'd ! Love, I fling up the game.
I choose, as a man should, a fresh hope and aim.
Will your cold little heart e'er admit its own blame ?
Till this hour it was idle to threaten retreat,
For life held no pleasure or pain half so sweet
As to lie here down-trodden beneath your dear feet.
    But perhaps even you to remorse may awaken
    When you learn I am slain, and that you are forsaken."

Cold in the Twilight.

(*Before Edgehill, October,* 1642.)

" Not always loom'd this bleak hillside,
    Seven years I toil'd with firm intent
To win for her, my plighted Bride,
    A home of peace and sweet content.
We loved, as few so well have loved,
    Afar or near, still faithful found ;
Each glad re-union but approved
    New flush of joy from cares' rebound.

" She was so fair, so fresh and true,
    So wholly mine in heart and soul,
Love held her ever in my view
    As bound secure while time should roll.
Then came Rebellion's harsh despite,
    And sour'd my nature, fierce and cold ;
Still turn'd I to her eyes' mild light,
    Still smooth'd her soft fair locks of gold.

" More harsh the outer world appear'd ;
    Weak, baffled, touch'd by angry pride,
Though careless for myself, I fear'd
    The future for my darling Bride.
When moody fits of discontent,
    Or weary languor, throbs of pain,
Had made my brow be sternly bent,
    At least none heard my tongue complain.

" How meekly, patiently she bore
    My varying moods I need not tell ;
Some sweeter balm remain'd in store
    When grateful love to her would swell :
Brightly she listen'd, pleas'd and gay,
    Her girlhood's bloom at once return'd ;
The saddened fears all cast away,
    The slanderous whisperers from her spurn'd.

" Would that it had been ever so—
    Had she stood firm when they drew nigh
Whose bitter hate, shown long ago,
    Had curst our love by lip and eye !
The Tempters wove their poison'd web,
    They parted us—yea, still do part :
Since then, my life doth ebb and ebb,
    While breaks in loneliness her heart.

" Is it the dawn-streak o'er yon hill ?
    I seem to hear her voice cry ' Come ! '
Hark ! 'tis the clarion sounding shrill,
    And now the hurried beat of drum.
Comrade, your hand ! now hard and fast
    The Roundhead rebels press in sight.
God grant this struggle be my last :
    ' For Charles, our king ! Heaven guard the right ! ' "

Old Nol.

(*Two days before Naseby, June* 12, 1645).

" No one in sight, except you, Tom, and I ?
 Nobody after us ? Zooks, what a rush !
Safely we've sped again, not a stitch dry,
 Well our steeds carried us, straight through the crush.
Cut, slash, and pelt, not a moment to spare ;
 Quickly they rallied, but fleet as the wind
We clatter'd, and few of their bravest would dare
 To follow us singly, the gang left behind.

" Who could have dreamt of an ambush laid there ?
 Cleverly plann'd, let us own, but it fail'd.
Knave who clutch'd bridle I paid for his share ;
 You, my boy, settled the next who assail'd.
Not much that fellow who cut through my arm
 Is likely to boast of the feat, I'll be bound ;
Stick him up sentry, he'll give an alarm—
 Didn't he yell when he roll'd on the ground ?

" Tie it up tighter, lad : pschut ! how it bleeds !
 Not the last blood I shall shed for my king.
In for sharp work we are, whoever leads :
 Leg across saddle we'll soon again fling.
Let the steeds loose, they'll not wander away,
 Earn'd a good rest they have, aye, and a feed ;
Chuck half the loaf to my gallant old Bay !
 Where had we been, had he fail'd in my need ?

" Safe the despatches I hold in my breast,
 One slash was turn'd by the lead-seal, like buff ;
Look, how my blood soak'd through them, my best.
 Thus would I drain each vein freely. Enough !

Hate I to swagger like Parliament-men,
　　Boasting for ever 'the Lord's on our side!'
Had we their leader Old Nol with us, then
　　Gladly to victory we two might ride!

"Sick of their cant and rebellion am I,
　　Not a pulse fails in my heart for our man;
Yet I'll confess, since no list'ner is nigh,
　　We're going to ruin as fast as we can.
Give our lives bravely we shall, to the end;
　　(Too late to stay grief from mother and Moll!)
You and I hold the same faith, my young friend,
　　All might be well had we leader like Nol.

"Something true English, the dog! about him:
　　Rugged and honest, though on the wrong side.
Not like that venomous born-rebel, Pym;
　　Or bullying Purge-of-the-Presbyters, Pryde:
Hampden, the makebate, who shatter'd his arm
　　With pistol o'erloaded at Chalgrove, and fell;
Or swarthy Tom Fairfax, still foremost in harm:
　　Or Essex, who'll find his *solatium* in hell.

"None of them all fit a candle to hold,
　　None of them worthy to pull off his boot;
Cromwell's the leader, both prudent and bold,
　　Plays the right card, tho' he holds the wrong suit.
Were he with us, 'stead of Rupert the rash!
　　Were he safe guide of King Charles, not his foe!
Then, by St. George! we'd to victory dash—
　　But we've rested an hour, so onward let's go."

Prince Rupert's Last Charge.

(*Naseby, June* 14, 1645.)

"This day will right us, or ruin us all!
    Was the thought through many a mind that flash'd,
As we answer'd our gallant Rupert's call,
    And forward against the Roundheads dash'd.
Never a braver leader than ours
    Summon'd a readier handful of men;
Fierce in the onset, like falling towers,
    Or the cataract rushing through highland glen.

"Choicest of troops that King Charles had known,
    Proudly he view'd us at early morn,
Gave out his words in a ringing tone,
    Glared at the foe with embitter'd scorn.
Something of taunt he mutter'd low,
    To those who had counsell'd delay of fight;
For the enemies' forces they could not show,
    Whether join'd or dissever'd, till came the light.

"None who beheld them, resolved and grim,
    Quail'd for a moment with recreant fear:
Little we cared, while each life and limb
    We hazarded boldly, or there or here.
Gay as in sport, we had fronted Death
    Too often to blench when we saw him now;
Mantled in mist of our chargers' breath,
    As they toss'd their long manes across our brow.

" Whispers had sped of some council feud,
  Rupert himself would have changed our ground,
 He who of all men the firmest stood
  To encounter worst odds, wherever found.
 ' Give me my troop well in hand,' he cried,
  ' Let but the road be from pitfalls free,
Quagmire, or calthrops by traitor shied,—
  Through hailstorm of shot men will follow me.

" ' Darkness or daylight to them all is one,
  They spy a match-spark, tho' sight be dull ;
Trust them to crash through a wall of stone,
  Trust them to slash through a helm and skull.
Set but those psalm-singing curs in front,
  Ireton or Cromwell whichever it be,
And we ask but to bear the battle's brunt :
  To the jaws of hell they will follow me.'

" ' Draw back in force !' still counsel the wise,
  ' Double our strength holds the eager foe,
Gerrald will speedily come with supplies : '—
  But Rupert and prudence no kinship know.
So in the bright early sunshine of June,
  Ranged are we all, to win or to die ;
We pant with delight for the signal that soon
  Leads onward to glorious victory.

"Light are the mocking jests that we fling
    At the scowling Rebels who gather so strong,
And we raise a shout 'For Church and King!'—
    Drowning their psalm in a Cavalier song:
'Then hey for the flaunting Rhine-Palatine flag!
    And hey for the Royal-Standard that flies!
And ho for the tattered old Parliament rag,
    That shall trail in the dust before their eyes.'

"Sound high, sound clear, our clarion shrill!
    Now dash we resistless with horse and steel,
And crash into Ireton's line, and kill;
    Wherever we meet them they topple and reel.
Fiercer and faster our troopers ride,
    Keen in pursuit o'er the hill we have flown,
Scattering foemen now far and wide,
    Vain to withstand us: the day is our own!

"Who shall recall us, and bid us return
    Back in our strength from our conquering raid?
Rupert alone, when with horror we learn
    That his rashness once more has our cause bewrayed.
Oh! bravest and best, of the dauntless heart,
    That could dare and achieve, not turn and wait:
Had others, like thine, fitly done their part,
    They had saved Naseby field, and conquer'd Fate."

Left on the Battle-field.

(*Naseby, June* 14, 1645.)

"If 'twere to do again, who'd change?
    Not I, who lost, and pay;
Yet to lie dying here seems strange;
    Sad close of my last day!
I waken from my fever-dream,
    The dying 'neath the dead;
I hear men groan, the night-bird scream:
    I see the stars o'erspread.

"One hand I still can move, and feel
    My wounds are bound in frost;
I pluck from out my side the steel:
    How was the battle lost?
It comes to memory, onslaught fierce
    We made on Ireton's line:
When through my breast his sword did pierce,
    And on his helm broke mine.

"My staunch Black Bayard weighs across
    My crush'd and shatter'd limb;
We lie together, deep in moss;
    Sometimes my senses swim:
I close my eyes, there comes again
    The face I loved most dear;
Then throbs once more this burning pain,
    Again that groan I hear.

" Better to drowse away from life,
 To seek yon distant sky,
Than still rush on from strife to strife :
 It is not hard to die.
Could she, my Mabel, see me now !—
 She armed me for the fight—
I know she'd bend, and kiss my brow,
 I've earn'd it well.   Good-night ! "

Uae Uictis !

'Twixt Cord and Axe.

(After Philiphaugh, September, 1645.)

" They call us Traitors, for that we
 Are faithful to our lawful king !
This Parliament, supremely free,
 Bidding us bow to them, or swing.
Each pledge of plighted troth they break,
 Honour's just claims they falsify :
Are we such fools to covenant make
With canting knave and hissing snake,
 While we can wield a sword, or die ? "

Short Shrift.

How the Cromwellians disposed of their Prisoners.

(Basing-House, Hants, October, 1645.)

"Shot to-morrow at half-past eight!"
  Beggarly Roundheads, that's my fate!
  That's the end of all your prate!
  Well then, I have not too long to wait,
  And need not waste time by sitting late,
  Watching the stars from my prison grate,
  Or musing on knotty affairs of State,
  Where the King grows small, and *you* are great!

"Half-past eight?" and then to sleep!
  Malkin and Bess perchance may weep,
  While Harry's Mildred a prayer will keep
  For me, whom Nol calls 'a wandering sheep'—
  Because of such wolves I'd make clean sweep.
  They left me no flask for potations deep,
  But of sanctified Sermons a goodly heap!
  What, read them? I'd sooner to Charon leap."

A Study in Browne and Gold.

(Norwich, June 14, 1646.)

The air was full of troubled news,
    While an excited crowd,
Leaving their task of soleing shoes,
    Talk'd politics aloud ;
Each man resolv'd his creed to choose,
    Himself than Pope more proud :

In Norfolk, where keen discontent
    Had always found a home,
Driving to willing banishment
    Across th' Atlantic foam
Grim Puritanic churls, all bent
    On warfare stern with Rome.

Still, the harsh bigots left behind
    Kept wrangling fierce and fell ;
Denouncing, in their rancour blind,
    Friends who had serv'd them well :
The sage divines of cultur'd mind,
    Against whom they rebel.

High as above gaunt huts and halls
   Their Norwich spire doth soar,
So rose one man above their brawls;
   He, the Physician, wore
No outward emblem that appals,
   Of mystic old-world lore.

Untainted by the world, he knelt,
   And mused, with heart at ease;
Concocting drugs that nauseous smelt,
   But cured each foul disease;
Apart from warring sects he dwelt,
   And pocketed his fees.

Unshaken amid social jars,
   Grave studies he pursued;
Healing slight hurts that leave no scars
   From paltry civic feud,
Or wounds from deadly civil-wars,
   With equal placitude.

Not that he scorn'd the rabble rout;
   He simply held his choice
To live in peace, to solve each doubt,
   And in his soul rejoice:
Deaf to the factions' vengeful shout,
   He heard sweet Wisdom's voice.

D

Men raved, men roar'd, as though the end
　　Of all things were at hand ;
·He would nor breath nor time expend
　　Their rant to understand :
He was too much their guide and friend
　　To be himself unmann'd.

" No call have I to grasp the sword,
　　Or to lay waste and slay ;
From tub or pulpit not one word
　　Am I inspired to say :
Yet can I work, and praise the Lord,
　　Content in mine own way."

Two centuries since then have sped ;
　　Calmly we now survey
The solemn nations of the dead,
　　Who warred in that old day :
And *his* the name most cherished,
　　That never fades away.

' *Thomas Browne, Armiger, Norfolcensis, obiit* 1682, *ætatis* 77.'

Waiting for the Dawn.

(Earth-Fort on Medway, Kent, May, 1648.)

" So, one more chance forspent, brave lad !
    We're trapp'd, our comrades flee ;
  You smile, and face the worst ? I'm glad
    Again that smile to see ;
  Aye, blow your match : at early morn
  We'll show Black Tom his gang we scorn.   *[Fairfax.*

" Only we two to hold the fort !
    The ill-plann'd sortie fail'd ;
  Long had our rations here run short,
    I knew the cowards quail'd :
  Since when, at dusk, the noisy pack
  Rush'd forth, not one of them comes back.

" I lash'd our standard round the staff,
    You rais'd it with firm strain ;
  At dawn we'll set it free, and laugh
    To hear their yells again :
  One shot apiece we keep in store,
  To greet the foes, no prime-pinch more.

" Well, Jack, the end draws closely nigh,
    We soon must use cold steel ;
  Stand back to back ! we thus can die :
    Time first, even now, to kneel,
  Before our lives away we fling,
  We pray God bless and guard our King."

A Cavalier's Grave.

(*Colchester, surrendered August* 28, 1648.)

He who lies this turf below
Willing was to stay or go,
Faced the worst, and scorn'd his foe :
Never until life should end
Lost his faith in king or friend,
Trusting still that times would mend.
Strong, resisting evil Power,
Cheerful in the darkest hour,
Prison-cell like Beauty's bower ;
With each humour could accord
Rosy wreath or statesman's word,
Poet's pen or warrior's sword.
Witness all those lays he sang !
Witness all the shouts that rang
His proud name 'mid battle clang !
  Wheresoe'er he came, he threw
  Freshen'd hope and impulse new :
  For all felt the man was true.

When at last by traitors' guile
He was snared, accounted vile,
At their malice he could smile ;
Look'd each ruffian in the face,
But disdain'd to ask for grace,
Though no help his eye could trace.
Vain were threats or bribes to move
Heart so stout, that would reprove
Those who mesh of Treason wove ;
Calm he stood, and bade them tell
Rebel troopers to aim well
At his breast : and thus he fell.
Glorious, as on battle-field,
Such a death his whole life seal'd :
Firm to die, but ne'er to yield.
Church and Crown are worth the cost :
Though awhile our cause be crost,
Surely nought of good is lost.
Where our stalwart Cavalier
Died a martyr, brave, sincere,
Rebel cowards, crawl not near !
    Bones may crumble into dust,
    But his soul is safe in trust
    For the Heaven that 'waits the Just.

The Cavaliers of Old.

(Chiddingstone, Kent, September 28, 1648.)

" I think there were few happier homes than ours,
　　Ere the grim puritans Rebellion preach'd ;
My youth pass'd like a dream in Winston-Towers,
　　Where all the land, so far as their sight reach'd,
Had to my sires belong'd : land held in trust
For those who found us lavish, kind, yet just.

" In quiet industry our cotters dwelt,
　　Simple their wants, supplied so soon as known ;
Sturdy and honest, men who ne'er had felt
　　A sense of wrong, till discontent was sown
By crop-hair'd curs who stealthily then came
To prate of public rights, and curse our name.

" Where had my father fail'd to help the poor ?
　　Each child was taught to worship God and pray ;
Each maid was rear'd in purity, secure,
　　Lest she might hapless fall the spoiler's prey ;
Claims of the aged ne'er were disallow'd :
The lowly murmur'd not, or deem'd us proud.

" My brothers mark'd the gathering of the storm,
 That broke too soon on our afflicted land;
While I lay nestled in illusions warm,
 Pored over books, or future travels plann'd :
Left to myself, to rove unwatch'd and free,
In boundless Chase or silent library.

" Our grey-hair'd Chaplain, whom all lov'd, would lead
 My thoughts to deeper studies than old rhymes
Of Ben and Beaumont, when he bade me read
 Records of heroes true of earlier times ;
Their faith in God, their loyalty to king :
He taught me more than I to practice bring.

" When I look back, remembering happy days,
 I see the sun-glints cross the polish'd floor ;
In nooks on helm and hauberk the light plays ;
 Shadow'd, the stately portraits frown once more :
My sister Maud sings gaily at my side,
While our own father smiles on us with pride.

" Maud, my young sister, who at Dijon sleeps !
 Strong are our girls in loyal faith, they scorn
Alliance with the rebels ; she who weeps,
 Falters, then weds a Roundhead, was not born
True Cavalier. Our women held more pride :
They broke false ties, spoke bravely, fled, or died.

"There's not a stone left now of Winston-Towers;
    The grand old woods, laid waste with axe and flame !
Freely we gave up all that once was ours,
    '*For Church and Crown*,' ungrudging loss or shame.
Some fell on scaffold, some on battle-field :
With sword we sign'd bequests, with blood we seal'd.

"None now remain of us, save I alone,
    The weakest and the youngest of the race ;
Little have I to hope for, who have grown
    Soldier of fortune, hunted from place to place.
You ask my life, in this last desperate Rise ?
Will it save the king ?—I seek no better prize."

E.

The Thirty-first of January.

(*Near Godalming, Surrey,* 164⅞.)

" How can I tell him ? Let me pause awhile,
    To gather strength and courage, for I seem
Smitten through heart and brain, although I smile
    Defiant at the future.   Do I dream ?
Or is it true, that I was call'd to hear ?—
    I, the last daughter of Sir Ralph Delaynes,
Who lies sore stricken, almost on his bier,
    Gazing for hours across our forfeit plains.

"The ruthless Trooper on his foaming steed
    Came with the tidings; ' Ho ! malignant race,
Vengeance is from the Lord ! Soon shall ye bleed,
    As bleeds your hated master.   On his face
Lie dust and ashes.   He, the Man of Blood,
    Was done to death at Whitehall, yesterday ;
Offer'd as Sacrifice : he who withstood
    The righteous arms Jehovah sent to slay.'

" Murdered ! Can it be true ?   Could rebels dare
    Affront the heavens with such a bloody deed ?
O Charles, our King ! Discrown'd thy head and bare,
    The head we honour'd, yet must thou too bleed ?
And I am but a woman, could not go
    To fling my life as free gift in the cause
I laid to heart, striving to crush the foe
    Of Sovereignty, of Church, and rightful laws.

" I knew our Cause was doom'd, from the first day.
    When the Flag waved at Nottingham, L'Estrange
Bore in his helm my Lute-string, laughing gay,
    And wore it still at Chalgrove.   Sad the change !
It came back to me, dash'd with drops of blood,
    His own heart's blood, they told me ; mine was chill'd.
Your tears, dear Mother, fell like Winter flood :
    I could not weep for him, my hero, kill'd.

" Then Arthur, my own brother, was shot down.
    Foremost with Rupert's best at Marston-Moor
He had rode gallantly for Church and Crown ;
    Pride of our house, brave as our sires of yore :
Cunning of fence, stalwart and strong of arm,
    Resistless where his charger clove the way
Through serried ranks of foemen, rebel swarm !—
    Till crush'd and helpless on the field he lay.

" They bore his body homeward, bore him here,
 Where all his happy days of youth were spent ;
I cleans'd his pale sad brow, but shed no tear,
 I kiss'd his sweet cold lips, and felt content.
He died as men should die, face to the foe ;
 Freely gave life, not sold it. Then I crept
Swift to my father's room, and bade him know
 The fate of his first-born. 'Twas he who wept.

" We were not those who shrink before the storm :
 One spirit ruled us, loyal to the death.
My hand was clasp'd by hand as firm and warm,
 Upon my cheek I felt my brother's breath.
To me he told his purpose : Could he stay,
 While thus Rebellion proudly rear'd its crest ?
For him I begg'd our father to give way,
 And send him forth, his youngest and our best.

" So all the varying fortunes of the war
 We track'd through rumour and false news or true ;
While many a Cavalier, with many a scar,
 Brought tidings from the field, and welcome knew.
Then a long silence follow'd, hard to bear ;
 Then swoop'd down on us all the bitter brood,
Who told us, ' Life were forfeit, but we spare ! '
 And robb'd us, preaching Scripture while they stood.

" I knelt one morning at my father's bed—
    Do you remember, three sad years ago ?
Did my voice tremble, Mother ? while I said,
    ' Give me your blessing, Father, ere I go !
Algernon lies in prison, wounded sore,
    And I must hasten ere it be too late ;
I do not dread the journey, or the more
    Than bitter converse through his dungeon-grate.'

" They told me he would die : they told me truth.
    Their words struck home, but still I urged my prayer.
Dark in the loathsome cell he lay, poor youth !
    Famine and fever left their death-seal there.
His wounds, untended long, I strove to heal,
    Cheering his heart, but swift the sand-grains sped.
His captors laugh'd ; they prais'd their Commonweal,—
    That crushes life, and desecrates the dead.

" No solemn rites, no mourners, scarce a shroud !—
    For had he not fought bravely for the king ?
' Nought to " malignants " could be here allow'd ;
    Into the pit such carrion vile we fling !'
Their words burn in my memory.   These the men
    That sought to slay King Charles, whom Scots had sold :
Scots, whom he once had crost, yet trusted then ;
    The Judas race traffic'd their King for gold.

" Slow years crept on : our Agnes droop'd and quail'd,
    Hers was the gentler heart, that broke, not bent ;
For in her silent misery reason fail'd,
    Before the sadly wasting life was spent.
So we two women watch'd her, each in turn,
    We could not bear to let a stranger know,
Till the fierce fires of phrensy ceas'd to burn :
    Then, at my call, our father totter'd slow.

" He held her hand in his, when the end came :
    The light of reason lit once more her eye,
Then lovely grew her smile, no word of blame
    Reproach'd our wrongers ; sorrow had gone by.
I think she saw, what none of us could see,
    That some one leant above her, for she rais'd
Her other hand, now clasp'd eternally
    In His Who never fails us.   God be prais'd.

" So closed her eyes in peace.   Ah ! happy she,
    Whom pain no more could drag from heights of prayer.
Oft in the twilight her dear face I see,
    Without one stain of earthly sorrow there.
I heard her voice sound clearly in the dark,
    Bidding me grieve no more, ' the close is near :'
And she awaits our early coming.—Hark !
    My father stirs within.   Did you not hear ?

" It cannot be, that he already knows ?
    Nay, 'tis impossible, and need must be
That now with the dread tidings I should go :
    There are none left with him save you and me.
Those whom of old we fed, as foemen stand ;
    Till all was stript from us, we freely gave ;
Melted the plate, parted with house and land :
    Surrender'd our lost darlings to the grave.

" Where may I turn and hide my anguish now,
    While tears and sobs burst quivering from me fast ?
Already the fierce pain thrills through my brow ;
    And this, the heaviest sorrow, comes the last.
How can we tell him Charles our King is slain ?
    Still must I be the messenger of woe ?
My cup brims o'er.   I cannot speak again—
    No, *this* to tell him, Mother, you must go."

One Year after Worcester Fight.

(*Bruges, September* 3, 1652.)

" If I knew where the laughing damosel dwelt
  Who smiled through her tears when we met, *that* day,
  And toss'd me a flower—while I mockingly knelt—
  As the wind from a wave tosses back the spray,
  (See! here are the leaves round the wither'd stem!
  Worn close to my heart, in her own dropt glove;)
  I would give my seal-ring, last hoarded gem,
  Could I whisper to her one word of love.

" Ladies I've bent to, in Court and hall,
  Dazzlingly fair with their queenly pride;
  Look'd in their eyes, and seen myself small,
  As they look'd in mine, and felt smaller beside;
  But some way it comes that the startled maid
  Whom I met on the hill, when my horse fell lame,
  Blooms fair like a hope, with all else decay'd:
  For I've little left now save a stainless name.

" Where can I find her?   A year has pass'd,
  I am here an exile on foreign shore;
  I scarcely dare dream that a thought can last
  In her breast, of the meeting we had of yore.
  She knew I was wounded, in flight, and poor,
  Yet she gave me fresh courage that conquer'd pain;
  Her smile and her flower proved Love's best cure:
  I'll not die till I show her this Rose again."

On the Shore of Loch Foyle.

(*Madge Edomal, non oubliée*, 1653.)

"In the calm of a Summer gloaming,
    When shadows are creeping slow,
Old memories waken, roaming
    Through the dreams of long ago.
I think of her, silently musing
    In the twilight far away,
Nestled close to her mother, losing
    The care that had pain'd by day.

"A gentle maid, and a fearless,
    With those quiet ways that hide
The strength of a virtue peerless
    Men seek in their chosen Bride;
Calm, amid stir and trouble;
    Firm, where the worldlings yield;
One who life's joys can double
    For those whom she comes to shield.

" Is she moving, a graceful presence,
 In the home of the sick and sad,
With Beauty's mysterious essence
 Making them strong and glad ?—
Does her voice, where music lingers,
 Speak comfort and heavenly peace ?—
Do her slender helpful fingers
 Smoothe the brow, till throbbings cease ?

" From her eyes are others learning
 What they earlier taught to me,
How they soothe rebellious yearning,
 And from bondage set us free ?—
While she went with smiles pursuing
 Whatever was right and true,
Unselfish, for others doing
 What they scarcely prized or knew.

" Thus I think of her still, and wonder
 If her thoughts yet turn to me,
Self-exiled, and held asunder
 From my darling across the sea.
Life is sad, but no fate may sever
 Firm friends who can trust and love :
Though hands may not clasp for ever,
 Heart meets heart in God's time, above."

A Wayside Tale.

After the 'Malignant' Cavalier ladies were dispossest.

(*Dormers-Green, Kent,* 1654.)

When first she came to Dormer's-Green
    Boys used to mock her garb uncouth ;
Her soul's true beauty was unseen
    By peevish eld or giddy youth.

Making no moan, no vain demur,
    She let the idle din go past ;
And smiled, as though One smiled on her :
    They learnt to love her well at last.

Winter came early and severe,
    She saved men from the prison door,
Warming their homes with Christmas cheer ;
    She won the blessings of the Poor.

When child or woman went astray,
    And every other voice spoke blame,
She strove to guide the holier way,
    And cloak'd with charity their shame.

When fever raged in squalid lanes,
    With cooling drink and noiseless tread
Her task was still to soothe all pains,
    And guard the orphans of the dead.

Where sorrow smote, where burdens bent,
  She soothed their grief with tender care ;
Teaching them patience and content :
  A welcome met her everywhere.

Joy won her sympathy, as well
  As sorrow : she could hear and smile
When bashful Love of hope would tell,
  Unveiling modest worth the while.

Childhood was glad to sport around
  Her chair, or cling to either hand ;
What time delight for them she found
  In hymns of the fair Morning-Land.

And thus erelong from old, from young,
  Or sad or gay, from high and low,
Arose her praises, freely sung,
  Nor knew she in the world a foe.

All now see beauty in her face,
  That oft had lighten'd human care ;
A Stranger, taking lowliest place ;
  An Angel, harbour'd unaware.

Old Ironside's Daughter.

(Forest of Dean, Gloucestershire, April, 1655.)

Puritan maiden, demure and shy,
Who is this Cavalier standing by?
Surely no brother of thine, I swear!
Swarthy is he, but thou art fair.
Sweet is the arch of thy dainty brow,
A glimpse of blue eyes I caught just now—
Blue as the skies that above thee shine:
His dark sad orbs are searching through thine.

Puritan maiden, thy voice sounds low,
Thy answering words come faint and slow;
His are not loud, so I cannot hear
The whisper that seems to be growing dear.
A rose-flush is spreading across thy cheek;
Thy fingers entwine round his, whom they seek:
It cannot be fancy that on his breast
Thy head sinks, like one who should be caress'd.

Puritan maiden, thy slender waist
By his other arm is gently enlaced ;
So far as I see, thou art nowise loth :
Happiness shines in the eyes of both.
Where is thy father ? who did commend
For thy future helpmate his 'trusty friend
Jabesh Saul Micklethwaite,' thumper of Tub :
Ere he believe them, his eyes he will rub.

Puritan maiden, true Prophet am I :
Thou shalt be won, and right speedily.
Vainly may Jabesh Saul snuffle, and whine :
Here is another voice blending with thine !
Thou art apt scholar, to hear him teach
Of a heaven more fair than the Roundheads preach ;
Thy horoscope shows to my learned 'quest
That thou choosest the man who can love thee best.

A Lay of the Tea-Drinking Roundhead.

(Sir Wilfull Lawless, at Coventry, in loco pænitentiæ, January, 1656.)

"A naughty world it is, my friends,
And naughty Drink men swim in;
An evil fate on those attends
Who turn to Wine or Women.
Such saintly crew as *I*-and-you
Much nobler bliss would seek up;
Cavaliers true we must undo,
So pass around the Tea-cup! . .

"Since social jars we love, not stars
And matters scientifical,
All Exploration-schemes or wars
To us are quite horrifical.
Learning we hate, and those who prate
Of grip or word of Mason:
Bœotian gloom to us gives room,
So pass the sugar-bason!

"We head a new slip-slop Crusade,
As Godfrey once 'gainst Saladin,
Denouncing each unrighteous blade
Who brings a flask or ballad in.
Our "Good Old Cause" needs crude rude Laws,
Till vines and fig-trees we earn;
Peal self-applause to our wise-saws:
Then pass around the Tea-Urn!

My Lady.

(In Exile, Brittany, S. Valentine's Day, 1656.)

" Things had gone wrong, full many a time,
　　Somewhat I fidgetted, somewhat storm'd ;
Often reliev'd my small mind with rhyme,
　　Cooling my wrath while the verses warm'd ;
Felt a few tremors, like growing old,
　　But quietly laugh'd, and refused to fret :
The years have grown better since first I told
　　My secret of love to Little Fanchette.

" Likely enough, there are troubles in store,
　　Our journey through life may be rugged still ;
Bringing few friends, though of foes a score,
　　Oft lacking means, when we cherish good will :
Sickness and poverty may attend,
　　Scorn and stupidity vex us, or debt :
But gaily I smile, as my way I wend,
　　If still companion'd by Little Fanchette.

" The world and its minions I hold pretty cheap,
　　The summer-sky friendship that hails Success,
Or the bleating applause which silly sheep
　　Yield when some favourite wolf they bless.
But I learn how idle it is to rave,
　　And be over-wise for a senseless set,
Railing because of each tyrant or slave :
　　While happiness waits me with Little Fanchette."

Kathleen.

(*E.K.A., Anno Domini* '57.)

I.

I count it not a grief that standing here
At the last verge of youth—while all around
Are busied with the duties they have found,
   With home-affection in each separate sphere—
   For me no smiling houschold-gods appear,
No voice of loving wife or children sound,
But like a Pilgrim wandering on strange ground
   I move unrestingly, year after year.
   Enough of joy to me, that as I go
Through windows of each dwelling I perceive
   True happiness enclasps the friends I know :
   Fortune or Fate can never be his foe
Who in another's bliss forgets to grieve,
   And with thanksgiving soars beyond his woe.

II.

Too much we sorrow for the things denied,
Too little prize the bounties freely strown,
That lost their charm when long familiar grown,
  Or seem'd more lovely benefit to hide ;
  Could I have felt so deeply, O fair Bride !
Had I not been myself on earth alone,
How blest shall be his hearth, how fond his tone,
  My olden friend, when thou art by his side ?
  And though no more, perchance, we two may meet,
Or seldom, in the years that yet must roll,
  To think in absence of thy bliss were sweet,
  Deeming thy wedded hours in brightness fleet ;
And, when at eve vague yearning fills the soul,
  One thought of me may cause true hearts to beat.

Sunshine.

(In the Dark Days of the Interregnum, '58.)

Can it be true that after weary pain,
Struggle and sorrow, dull cold apathy,
Harder to bear than grief, there flows to thee
   The sweet warm breath of Love yet once again ?—
   Sweeter and warmer than when some might feign
To smile in earlier days entrancingly,
Alluring to mad worship, could they see
   Themselves deem'd perfect, without fault or stain.
   Fairer than dreams foretold, behold her come,
True Sunshine ! yielding warmth and welcome here,
   Ready to share each fortune, good or ill:
   In whose calm presence the world's clang or hum
Ceases to deafen or perplex thine ear:
   While holier aims thy heart revive and cheer.

"Voila ma Vie!"

(A Cavalier's Creed, 1658.)

To him whose hardest toil seems play,
  Since well he loves his labour,
Life gives continual holiday,
  While Time plays pipe and tabor.

To him who on a crust can dine,
  With frugal sip of water,
Fortune sends gifts of cates and wine,
  Because—he never sought her.

Be modest in demands on Fate,
  Be thankful for small mercies;
And take what comes, or soon or late,
  With blessings, not with curses.

Regicide Gains.

(*Whitehall, August* 24, 1658.)

" It cannot be done ! " I heard him say,
  Muttering low in the dead of night,
Wild words, remember'd for many a day :
  " *Cannot we bury our dead out of sight ?*
Why do they haunt me, wherever I turn ?
  Straight in my path, when I onward haste ;
Oft at my couch, till my eyeballs burn :
  By the men whom I slew am I yet outfaced.

" What is my gain from the blood-stain'd years,
  If these ghastly spectres haunt me still ?—
I who have conquer'd all doubts and fears,
  Knowing no law save my ruthless will.
Scruples and qualms were for weaker men ;
  I could find my excuse in delusive right :
Foes were despoil'd and slain—but then,
  Cannot we bury the dead out of sight ?

" I know right well I could face the crowd
    Whom we massacred, and called it peace :
We stifled the voices that cursed us loud,
    Though clamour is bitter, it soon must cease.
But the face of each foeman whom living I knew
    Confronts me, and thrills : each sever'd head
With blood slowly dripping, with pallid hue :
    The accusing whispers I hear, and dread.

" Preach to me comfort, and tell me ' no sin
    Can leave stain on the soul of the Lord's Elect ; '
Quench the fierce fires that are burning within ;
    Help me forget the lives I have wreck'd :
Give me new strength, for I dare not die
    With my name accurst, my life one blight.
Shall I see murdered Charles when in grave I lie,
    Even there, and for ever, to haunt my sight ? "

End of the Usurpation.

(*Interregnum, May,* 1660.)

Not dim and shadowy, like a world of dream,
  We summon back the past Cromwellian time,
  Rais'd from the dead by invocative rhyme,
Albeit this no *Booke of Magicke* seem :

Now, while few questions of the fleeting hour
  Cease to perplex, or task th' unwilling mind—
  Lest party-strife should better reason blind
To th' evils waiting still on despot Power.

We see Old England torn by civil-wars,
  Oppress'd by gloomy zealots—men whose chain
  Gall'd worse because of Regicidal stain,
Hiding from view more honourable scars.

We see how those who raved for Liberty,
  Claiming the law's protection 'gainst their King,
  Trampled themselves on Law, and strove to bring
On their own nation tenfold slavery ;

So that with iron hand, with eagle eye,
  Stout Oliver Protector scarce could keep
  The troubled land in awe : while mutterings deep
Threaten'd to swell the later rallying cry.

Well had he probed the hollow friends who stood
   Distrustful of him, tho' their tongue spoke praise ;
   Well read their fear, that interposed delays
To rob him of his meed for toil and blood.

A few brief years of such uneasy strife,
   While foreign shores and ocean own his sway ;
   Then fades the lonely Conqueror away,
Amid success, weary betimes of life.

So passing, kingly in his soul, uncrown'd,
   With dark forebodings of approaching storm,
   He leaves the spoil at mercy of the swarm
Of beasts unclean and vultures gathering round.

For soon from grasp of Richard Cromwell slips
   Semblance of power he had not strength to hold ;
   And wolves each other tear, who tore the fold,
While lurid twilight mocks the State's eclipse.

Then, from divided counsels, bitter snarls,
   Deceit and broken fealty, selfish aim—
   Where courage with prompt action win the game—
Self-scatter'd fall they : and up mounts KING CHARLES.

Entr'Acte.

Once more our mimic curtain draws aside,
   Showing the Lovers both of court and city;
Not quite the damsels you might seek as Bride,
   Too free in speech, though lively, arch, and witty ;
But, to my mind, nice nymphs to sit beside,
   Whispering in turn, for they look young and pretty :
As for the men, gay, reckless, oft decried—
   If you dislike their company, more's the pity!

E.

Cavalier Lyrics.

PART II.—RESTORATION TO REVOLUTION.

Pause not too long, fair Reader, turn the page !
It gives our Second Part to thy attention ;
Though we abjure the Commons in dissension,
  And war against the harsher Sectaries wage :
Yet politics need not awaken rage,
While of Divines and Beauties we make mention,
With Poets, fed or starved, quick at invention :
  These, her fit subjects, may our Muse engage.

No scent of gunpowder we now perceive,
  But courtlier perfume (sometimes no less deadly),
Where Shaftesbury intrigues would round him weave,
  While scandal track'd Bab Palmer and Kate Sedley :
' Old Rowley' comes, ere he doth take his leave,
  Smiling amused at Life's discordant medley.

F

[*⁎* A fragment of a genuine Post-Restoration ditty is extant, in *Roxburghe Ballads*, v. p. 83, celebrating "*The Merry Boys of Christmas*," and beginning, "Come, come, my roaring ranting boys, let's never be cast down : We'll never mind the Female Toys, but loyal be to th' Crown." They seem to have loved their Christmas Beer, "not wisely, but too well," like Othello. Each laid him bare-faced on his beer, as the white-headed person of whom the fair Ophelia sang ; and Queen Gertrude practically commented thereafter, "The drink, Hamlet, the drink." She knew it to be attractive, and was quick to take it. So was Lady Macbeth, hot ; for she not only habitually prepared the toddy— "Go, bid your mistress, when my drink is ready, she sound upon the bell ! "—but confessedly was made " bold " in Dutch-courage by sharing the tipple that overmastered Duncan's grooms. Truly at Shakespeare's hospitable board, " it snewed in his house of meate and drinke."

On our pp. 68 and 69 we give six substitutionary stanzas for the lost continuation of the fragment mentioned above, *loc. cit.*

" The Figure of 2 " was a well-understood allusion to King Charles the Second, during the Interregnum, and it was symbolized by the woodcut, copied below. To this phrase a reference is made on p. 71.]

The Twenty-Ninth of May, 1660.

" *We have welcom'd King Charles home again !*
   And can pass, when our time come, content ;
 Forgetting old sorrows and pain,
   Or accounting them blessings well meant.
 We have seen him, all eyes on him bent,
 Bright with hope, each heart loving and gay :
   Thus for long years one cry shall be sent,
 ' *All be merry, this Royal-Oak-Day !* '

" *How he smiled, when the maids scatter'd flowers,*
   Though they were but to carpet his feet ;
 Amid oak-leaves festoon'd, like Love's bowers,
   Stood our fairest of Dames, blooming sweet ;
   Then, his Triumph the more to complete,
 Came the grandsires, feeble and grey,
   To welcome their King, as was meet :
 ' *All be merry, this Royal-Oak-Day !* '

" *Thus Restored, he felt joyous to find*
   No murmur or scowl from his foes ;
 His words were most gracious and kind,
   Widely sprent, as the Husbandman sows
   The good seedling corn, that he throws
 In his generous abundance away ;
   Loyal spilth fetches harvest, he knows :
 ' *All be merry, on Royal-Oak-Day !* ' "

L'Envoi.

Prince, we welcome you home, full of faith
   That no chill Winter follow bright May :
 We list one voice alone, and it saith,
   " *All be merry, this Royal-Oak-Day !* "

Restoration Health to the King, 1660.

(To the favourite Cavalier Tune of, *Hey, boys, up go we!*)

" Drink we a health to Charles our King,
 And his royal brother James !
Welcome them home : their praise we sing,
 While high the bon-fire flames.
No canting conventicler Saint
 Need join us in good cheer ;
Mince-pies, plum porridge, make him faint :
 He sours our Christmas-Beer.

" What time those hypocritick knaves
 Denounced our harmless joys,
They silenced all the Loyal staves
 Chorus'd by Roaring Boys.
Men bore the yoke, in doleful dump,
 Waiting this happier year ;
When Monk came south, we burnt ' the Rump,'
 And drank our Christmas Beer.

" Then let's rejoice, the day's our own,
 No more ' the Saints ' shall reign ;
Phanaticks shall not bear us down
 With '*Forty-one* again.   [*i.e. 1641.*
We've had enough Jack-Presbyters,
 And 'Pendents swaggering here :
A murrain on the Roundhead curs !
 Boy, bring more Christmas-Beer."

The Milk-Maid's New-Year Answer.

(To the same favourite Cavalier Tune of, *Hey, boys, up go we!*)

"Ho! Merry Boys, who Christmas keep
    A week or more together,
Who quaff and sing, but never sleep,
    Whatever be the weather,
We Milk-maids scorn, this New-Year Morn,
    To taste your vaunted cheer;
Our cans hold drink more sweet than horn
    Of ranting roarers' Beer.

"For shame! ye rail at 'Female Toys,'
    Because on sots they frown;
Men who can prize no rural joys
    Must rake and scoff in town.
We are up before the Winter Sun
    Doth in the East appear;
Before he set, our toils are done,
    While you swill Christmas-Beer!

"Take this, our New-Year Gift, and be
    More just to womenkind;
We are not proud, but frank and free,
    To Lads who hit our mind.
Come, help us lift our heavy pails,
    And call us 'fair' and 'dear':
We'll meet you then, next Whitsun ales—
    Though not with Christmas-Beer."

"Merry Drollery."

(*Cavalier Song-book*, 1661, 1670.)

"Merry and Wise" the proverb bade us be:
"Wise," ruled the saintly, "but by no means Merry!"
They straightway sought all joy to kill and bury.
 Marvel not then, if Cavaliers we see
 (By ample proof in antique *Drollery*)
Chose Mirth alone, quaffing too much of Sherry.

Merry and Wise! Welcome be smiles of youth,
On lips not yet in anguish blench'd and bitten;
Be sportive gambols of each lamb and kitten.
 He who would banish Mirth is scant of ruth:
 Why should grim visages repel from Truth?
Soon may each joyous heart be cold or smitten.

Merry and Wise! True text for books like ours
Which tell of troubled times, and men half frantic,
Drunk with a short-lived glee, playing their antic.
 Still seek we innocent mirth, and fragrant bowers,
 That show no reptile-slime upon the flowers:
Shun Mirth that soils, and Wisdom grown pedantic.

Becalmed.

(Greywell Hill, Hampshire, 1662.)

" No, no, I say, not another drop !
  I love liquor well, but know when to stop,
  And two pottles of white have fill'd my crop,
      Not to mention one of red ;
  So, were there no risk of the term ' milk-sop,'
      I should trundle off to bed.

" What ! turn to the fire, and talk ?—why not ?
  Let us drain a fresh bowl of something hot ?
  This is not like Rose-tavern, to pay our shot,
      And then tramp out to the cold :
  I'm the guest of a friend, in his happy lot,
      Who remembers the days of old.

" Hard times we have both of us seen, good lack !
  Since at Naseby our swords did the rebels hack,
  But we 'scaped the doom of tribunal black,
      When my brother Will was slain ;
  Till at last 'the Figure of Two' came back,   [*Charles II.*
      And *he* got his own again.

" So home came we, with many a score,
  Who had roved abroad from door to door
  In sorriest plight, reckless and poor,
      Ragged as half-pluck'd crows ;
  Hoping perhaps that our deeds of yore
      Had won us at least repose.

" But the truckling thieves had taken root
  In each Naboth's vineyard, gorged with fruit ;
  To lop them, or dig out the gang, did not suit
    The Convention coblers at all :
  We had suffer'd wrongs, with taunts to boot,
    And on wounded stumps might crawl.

" Not an acre or barn that once was mine
  Could be wrench'd from the maw of the greedy swine
  Who had butcher'd the king, and despoil'd his line
    Of rights in the twelve past years ;
  They now ' drank to Charles ! ' in the plunder'd wine
    Of his outcast Cavaliers.

" Yes, they drank, by St. George ! and dropt the mask ;
  Their puritan cant grew a weary task ;
  Now they ' hated Nol Brewer, and spurn'd his cask :'
    They ' had always pray'd for the King ! '
  'Twas good done by stealth ! they now would bask
    In Court sunshine, like grigs, and sing.

" At Whitehall they cluster'd (the knaves !) to stare
  At a shabby old cloak like mine, thread-bare,
  Alongside the turn'd coats, belaced and fair,
    Which the newly-made-loyal wore :
  Our Rupert's men once might drink and swear,
    But, ye gods, how the Saintly swore !

" So 1 soon grew sick of the bootless quest
    After scraps of largesse, doled to the rest,
    And I came where my Mildred lies cold in the West,
        Half weary to lie there too ;
    For life look'd tarnish'd and shrunken, unblest :
        When by luck I chanced on you.

" And you, old comrade, had found your nook,
    Had changed your sword to a Pastor's crook ;
    But you welcomed me here, when all else forsook,
        In your Hampshire hermitage :
    And now you are happy, 'twixt bride and book,
        Letting faction go scheme or rage.

" When I found fresh flowers on Mildred's grave,
    Where the darkening boughs of cypress wave,
    Could I guess whose remembrance that token gave
        Of his love for Mildred's child ?
    Well, there's nothing in life for myself I crave,
        Since Fortune this once has smiled.

" It feels like awaking from troubled sleep,
    To sit here now, while the minutes creep,
    Tick'd softly by clock-beat ; to know you keep
        Your friendship so true and warm.
    And my daughter's your wife ! I'm a fool to weep,
        But—she's harbour'd safe from the storm."

A Wasted Life.

(Cavalier Vigil at Royal-Oak Hostelry, October, 1664.)

" Bring me another flask, good Will !
    And trim the lamp that's giving warning ;
Heap on fresh logs, the night grows chill :
    No need to stir me hence till morning.
My loft is lonely, and I dread
    The ghosts that lurk in time of trouble ;
So you may rest you on your bed,
    And leave me here till I see double.

" My comrades all have sought their homes,
    Black looks await them from their spouses ;
Soon addled were their wits, poor momes !
    With drink that scarce my spirit rouses.
Dull cits are they, who good hours keep,
    And must to business hasten early ;
Eager to drowse their brains with sleep,
    Then, if their conscience prick, turn surly.

" Little of sympathy they feel
    For such a royster as they know me ;
No scorn, if felt, need I conceal,
    For the scant courtesy they show me.
But I have lost my proper mates,
    Either ill-luck or self-will crost me ;
And, since blank solitude one hates,
    I pick up human crumbs thus tost me.

" One comfort, at the least, is left,—
　　They have no wit to understand me ;
While friends, of whom I am bereft,
　　Would sigh to see where Fate doth land me :
Scholar and wit in early days,
　　Renown'd as high as they at college ;
Then courtier, warrior, in the blaze
　　Of ladies' eyes and statesmen's knowledge.

" Was it my fault I fail'd, and fell
　　To this drear waste of life's mischances ?
Or was it, as I deem, her spell
　　That crush'd my hope ? her smiles and glances.
Whom have I loved, but her alone,
　　Who made me worship her, and trust her ?
Her voice, what witcheries in the tone !
　　Her eyes, no stars excell'd their lustre.

" Had I not lost her, still I ask—
　　Would not her life and mine be brighter ?
Without her, worthless seems each task—
　　Each prize, of ermine, sword, or mitre.
This, this alone yields me content,
　　That she who might have blest and made me,
Knows, as her own sole punishment,
　　She wreck'd my life when she betray'd me."

La Belle Stewart.

(*Westminster, March,* 1667.)

" I have seen her again, and I wonder no more
At the fame of her matchless beauty and grace :
That the wisest are dazzled, the youngest adore
The charm of her exquisite innocent face.
She moves with such stately refinement of mien,
Scarcely rustling the robes that float round her fair form ;
A bright smile comes like sunshine, avow'd as the Queen
Of hearts that are pure and unselfish and warm.

" There are no eyes like her's, softly lustrous and blue :
For a moment their gaze wanders far, far away,
As if seeking affection more honest and true
Than the frivolous Court-life can yield day by day.
Even there, some may prize her sweet nature, that ne'er
In scorn or in hatred flings word that can wound ;
Yet with one glance she awes, if bold Licence press near,
Like a harsh note discordant, with all else attuned.

" Shall I ever forget the first time she came here ?—
   A fair child, all her virginal beauty in bud—
   Somewhat timid and shy, yet with little to fear
   From the rillets of passion, now coursing in flood.
   Who could see the bright maid, newly truant from France,
   Where her father found refuge well earn'd by brave deeds—
   Who could see, and not hope the full ripen'd advance
   Of charms in the future, whatever heart bleeds ?

" It was omen of evil when proud Castlemaine
   Drew the blushing young nymph to her side, as a friend ;
   She whose eyes kindled fire, whose lips left a stain,
   Whose voluptuous allurements death only can end.
   Nought comes from her touch, save contagion and blame,
   Her thoughts are pollution, her words coarse and vile !
   We might shudder, and prophesy ruin and shame
   For the girl whom fiend Barbara greeted with smile.

" Yet she fell not from Virtue.   Each arrow that flew,
   Barb'd with passionate love 'gainst that bosom so rare,
   Was blunted and foil'd : her heart remain'd true :
   She was chaste and indifferent, ice-cold though fair.
   When lovers throng'd round her, their whispers oppress'd,
   She look'd weary, indignant, or laugh'd in reply ;
   She clapt hands like a child at some mountebank jest,
   But turn'd a deaf ear to each sonnet or sigh.

" Men might say, in requital, 'The creature's no mind,
No heart, no romance! why waste time on a fool?'
But, unless they discours'd with one hopelessly blind,
Or a rival repuls'd, 'the Court granted no rule!'
Talk was idle: her fingers kept building-up cards,
Like Châteaux d'Espagne, to a fabulous height,
While to patient skill'd helpers her smile she awards:
When her breath blew all down came supremest delight.

" Half-hidden 'mid curtains, or fenced in by chairs,
Our King Charles loved to prattle an hour or more
With his 'dearest fair Tyranness!' trying fresh snares
To entrap her to yield, like known wantons before:
While courtiers might titter, proud ladies would sneer,
And shrug their bare shoulders, wherefrom the lace fell;
George Villiers, flush'd, frowning, as jealous with fear,
Tried to listen to Wilmot's worst jibes, ill or well.

" To be theme of rude jests, to be toasted and prais'd
By the gayest of spendthrifts, was galling to pride:
There were tears in her eyes, the arch'd brows were rais'd,
And she dwelt in a desert, no friend by her side.
She was flatter'd and sought, for her influence great:
Lely caught her *parure*, her complexion and grace;
And Röttier the medallist, paid by the State,
Lost his heart while he modell'd her beautiful face.

" ' She shall live as *Britannia* while England holds sway,
With her clear perfect profile, her dignity rare!'
Well, though Beauty, thro' sickness and age must decay,
Let the sculptor and painter such merits declare.
Age, sickness !—who knoweth how soon they may wreck
All that gladdens the sight in ' La Frances, ma Belle,'
When the eyes that now thrill us, that rapturous neck,
Those lips that crave kisses, are dust :—Who can tell ?

" Was it something of terror foreshadowing this,
A dread of disease that still haunts London town,
Made her weary of Court, its temptation or bliss,
And long for safe shelter, a hind hunted down ?
To stay there, half dazzled, insulted with bribes,
She had learnt, was worse peril, her self turn'd her foe :
Was there no one so noble, among all the tribes
Of lordlings and matrons, to whom she could go ?

" Yes, the Queen, her own Mistress ! to her she appeal'd,
For protection, forgiveness, and told how one man
Made proffer of marriage : Her tears, while she kneel'd,
Attested her truth, since repentance began.
Duke Richmond, Charles Stewart, most gladly would win
Her hand—for her heart, oft refus'd, he had striven :—
She would fly from the Palace, its riot and sin,
To find peace as his bride. She was heard, and forgiven.

" To-night rose a storm, such as March winds can bring,
　The rain pour'd in torrents, the trees sway'd and fell ;
　There were messengers seeking for speech with the king,
　There were portents, disasters, and sad news to tell.
　'Mid the hurry and noise, past the sentry and guard,
　Unfearing the darkness, the wild swirling rain,
　'La Belle Stewart' escaped from foul Whitehall-Yard :
　Undaunted and pure, she won freedom again.

" It was something to live for, to see her this night,
　When I waited at Westminster here with her steed,
　Exchanged her drencht mantle, and saw her eyes bright
　In her triumph : she call'd me her ' true friend at need !'
　Not one moment to waste, since pursuit would be made,
　But her husband was waiting, the priest made them one ;
　They had kept their own counsel, no secret betray'd :
　And I knew both were happy while galloping on."

[*Note.*—He carried her off to Cobham Hall, near Gravesend, at the
end of March, 1667. One year later, as here foreshadowed, her beauty
was ravaged by small-pox, whereby one of her eyes was almost
destroyed, in March, 1668. Sir Peter Lely's portrait of her is earlier.
John Röttier's medallion, still extant at the British Museum, was
modelled in February, 1667, when she became the representative of
Britannia on our coinage. See the woodcut copies (on pp. 537 and 542
of vol. i.) in the truly excellent *Medallic Illustrations of the History of
Great Britain*, compiled by the late Edward Hawkins, printed by order
of the Trustees of the British Museum in 1885 : a book of great value.]

One-Acre Priory.

(Near the Weald of Kent, May 17, 1667.)

Mine is a very small domain,
　Where long I dwell with Nycis';
Few are our wants, of heart or brain,
　For both it well suffices,
As though it were Pacific Main
　With all its Isles of Spices.

Two Maids we keep, both young and fair;
　One cat, a famous mouser;
Some poultry, flowers, and a full share
　Of dogs (Spring, Elphin, Towzer) ;
With southern aspect, wholesome air:
　These suit an old carouser.

To envy others silly seems;
　Who wealth have, fain grow richer:
Books form my sole ambitious schemes,
　(Nycisca's flowers bewitch her):
Contentedly I weave my dreams,
　And lack nor Friend nor Pitcher.

O Grumblers of dyspeptic sort,
　Who count yourselves stupendous,
Why scorn a Lilliputian Court,
　Where simple joys attend us?
We thank the Gods, this life is short,
　Till the New Life they send us.

G

Memories and Forecast.

(Hampton-Court, after the Ball, 25 June, 1667.)

" Yes, 'twas unlucky. Broke your fan ?
    Trod on your skirt ? the clumsy man,
              Unfit for dances ;
    Spoilt your Court-Ball, that well began !
    No wonder now you rail and ban,
              With 'vengeful glances.

" Yet, hush ! in stillness of this eve,
    Idle it seems to mope and grieve
              Over past crosses ;
    Or call Fates cruel, that bereave ;
    Or try fresh schemes and wiles, to weave
              A cure for losses.

" Love, with fair brow thus knit, why lour ?
    Nature has lavish'd all her dower
              To make Earth pleasant ;
    So sit sedately here, in bower,
    And do not spoil the flitting hour,
              While June is present.

" Hereafter, if we must, my dear,
  When autumn leaves are turning sere,
          Yield we to sorrow ;
  Or Prudence, with her brow severe,
  May find us lend attentive ear,
          Perforce, to-morrow.

" But this is Love's own hour.   Too soon
  Our month will pass, and we change tune,
          Till Time renews it :
  From early dawn, through glorious noon,
  To stilly midnight, prize sweet JUNE,
          And grudge to lose it.

" So shall we boast, if e'er we see
  Dark days and sad—'neath leafless tree
          (Now green and sappy),
  Hearts chill'd by scorn and penury,
  Sinking in hopeless misery—
          ' *That* June was happy ! ' "

Our Undeserted Village.

(A Cavalier's Birthplace: London, 2nd September, 1667.)

" Would you know the supremest of pleasures,
  That the heart of a man could inspire,
Beyond Harems of Beauties, with treasures
  Of jewels and robes they desire ?—
'Tis to mingle, caress'd, and caressing,
  With Scholars and loveliest Dames,
Who together are drawn here, confessing,
  ' There's no place like our Village-on-Thames ! '

" I admit it has faults, flaws, and errors,
  (There are few perfect cities or men,)
But for me it possesses no terrors,
  Though 'twas awkward with Plague now and then ;
But since two years ago this is mended,
  When the foul alleys perish'd in flames,
And the sight last September was splendid
  Of our dear little Village-on-Thames.

" ' It arises a Phœnix ! ' (pshaw ! bathos !)
  ' Thanks to praiseworthy efforts ' (Kit Wren's) ;
But one can't weep in Palinode pathos
  For the burning of picturesque dens ;
Since our crowded blind-courts and quaint gables,
  Hanging roofs, which Wence Hollar now fames,
Kept imprison'd an odour of —— stables
  (And worse), in our Village-on-Thames.

" It might suit some coarse Hectors and wenches,
    Who through darkness each labyrinth search,
To enjoy the strong perfumes, call'd stenches,
    When they worship'd in taverns, not church :
For my part, like our monarch, ' Old Rowley,'
    With the litter of spaniels he names,
One may sniff and pass by ; nor breathe solely
    Rank fumes in our Village-on-Thames.

" As for gardens and walks, are there fairer
    Than those that our Temple displays ?
Are there groves of tall trees, flowers, rarer
    Than Hyde Park can offer for praise ?
While for buildings—compared with the Abbey
    (Though we burnt Old St. Paul's), what are claims
Of cathedrals and duomos, all shabby,
    To our own, in this Village-on-Thames ?

" We can land below bridge, find a bower,
    Where on cherries and cream we regale ;
We may dream of Queen Bess, near the Tower,
    Or amid foreign galleons may sail ;
Seeing warehouse and wharves in alliance,
    Or proud mansions no spider-web shames ;
No Bourse 'gainst our 'Change frowns defiance :
    What can equal our Village-on-Thames ?

" Here the best of each class is attracted,
    In refinement and culture to grow ;
All the world's various products compacted,
    Here transcendantly industries show ;
Fair Science and Art claim the student,
    While the idler finds folly and games :
At your choice you waste life, or are prudent,
    In our dear little Village-on-Thames.

" Ere you tempt me to Garden of Eden,
    You must bring back for me my lost Eve ;
"Twould be banishment—Iceland or Sweden—
    Were I once more my birthplace to leave.
Though I suffer'd sore exile, scant rations,
    Defeat of ambition, crost aims,
I enjoy'd changeful life in all nations,—
    But loved none like our Village-on-Thames.

" As we floated, this still Autumn twilight,
    On the breast of the river we love,
In a dream of hush'd rapture, that *my* light
    Always brings, with the stars faint above,
One thought of my darling consoled me—
    Outweighing all failures and blames—
Since that she too best loved (so she told me,)
    This dear little Village-on-Thames."

(E. S. B.)

(The Priory, June, '72).

The surface they scan, and think they know:
Little they guess of the depth below,
Or how swiftly the silent waters flow.

Here are no Minster aisles,
  No proudly swelling dome ;
Above the elms a grey church-tower
  Shadows my peaceful home.

No crowded street, where squalor begs
  From Folly or Disdain ;
But dark groves flecked with golden gleams,
  And many a greenwood lane.

Men say, " No guilt or pain
  Could touch one here : the bliss
Of Eden, ere a sin was known,
  Can but have equall'd this."

O darling, wert thou here !
  (Our dream of long ago) ;
Now, nought is won, since thou art gone :
  No wilderness more drear.

"One of the People called Quakers."

(18th day of Third Month in year '73.)

So passes, far from worldly strife,
　A spirit fervent, tried and true,
The Peace she loved in mortal life
　Waits her beyond the heavenly blue.

Not hers the choice of human praise,
　While to her ear the words could sound;
Now, humbly hush'd, no voices raise
　A Dirge to grace her burial-ground.

Here in this quiet resting spot,
　Where "The Friends" pay their modest rite,
Her dust is shrined, forgotten not,
　Though no proud tomb arrest the sight.

But here shall come, with reverent heart,
　Those who had known and loved her well;
Too strong in faith for tears to start:
　Content on lonelier earth to dwell.

No trump of fame may sound afar
　The virtues that her life adorn'd;
Fame blazons conquest, guilt, and war:
　Meek holiness keeps silent, scorn'd.

Yet sweeter shall the welcome be
  Whisper'd by angels from above,
Than all the unheeded eulogy :
  Crown'd as she is with Christian love.

Mother in Israel, peace be thine!
  We for ourselves bereft may sigh :
Thou, thou hast reach'd the Life divine ;
  We, though we seem to live, here die.

We need thy earnest faith, to quell
  The doubts that rise in troubled days ;
We need thy courage to dispel
  The darkness of our trodden ways.

We miss thy hand, thy guiding word,
  Now pass'd for ever, in our gloom :
O friend beloved, are whispers heard
  Rais'd by true love around thy tomb ?

We may not ask an answer given,
  A secret message, word or sign,
But we would strive to reach thy heaven
  By life that fain would copy thine.

So pass, from all our earthly care,
  To HIM Who loveth thee the best,
Whither arose thy life-long prayer :
  Pass, to the promis'd Home ; and rest.

The Blind Poet at Bunhill-Fields.

(*London, July* 23, 1673.)

"What made me speak to him at first ? (you ask)—
　　The grim old Puritan, whom you despise ;
' Who set himself to an ungrateful task,
　　And had to pay the forfeit with his eyes ? '
Friend, since you never met him, knew him not,
　　Or yet his writings, only his ill-fame,
I strive to plead with you for his hard lot,
　　Though I absolve him not from former blame.

"It was no chance that led me to his door,
　　While he dwelt sick and weary, sad at heart ;
I comforted my nurse, grown old and poor,
　　Whose dwelling stands from his three yards apart.
There, one long summer evening, when the sun
　　Had forced Annette to linger in the shade,
Close to his trelliss'd porch, as oft she'd done,
　　I heard sweet music on his organ play'd.

" Music, that seem'd to soar above our world,
    And bear me as on wings to purer skies :—
Ah! now I see with scorn your lip is curl'd ;
    You hate him, and forget his miseries.
You are wrong. I grant that he was harsh, austere,
    Of an unyielding temper, fierce in pride ;
Bitter reproofs have I been forced to hear—
    As when he drove his daughters from his side.

" A man whom few could love or hope to please,
    Opinionative, discontented, wont
To harbour cold suspicion like disease :
    One prone to take revenge for each affront.
What could he learn from that schismatic gang,
    With whom in Cromwell's dark days he shared power,
But their intolerance and envenom'd fang ?—
    Rebels who bit and snarl'd throughout their hour.

" Swiftly the shadows crept high up the wall,
    The last rays faded from the flowers, the glow
From heaven above, and night's funereal pall
    Enwrapt us, fill'd with solemn thoughts below.
For still that wondrous music swell'd and peal'd,
    Grand in its dauntless fervour ; then would wind
With tenderest sweetness round my heart, and seal'd
    As in a fount the thought—' O God ! he is blind ! '

" I could not speak, but silent went my way,
 Musing and wondering, to my sleepless bed,
Strangely awe-stricken ; to return next day,
 And cheer Annette, whose humble board was spread.
Gladly she told me, o'er the frugal meal,
 Of kindly acts that brought back gentle word
' From good John Milton :' doubtless he could feel
 The honest homage she must need afford.

" Ere long, before chill nights had closed us round,
 The week seem'd void if, by mischances crost,
My road to her trim garden was not found :
 Then ' Paradise' to me again was ' lost.'
I found his book laid open, read and loved
 The marvellous poem of that early pair,
Who in their stainless beauty unreproved
 In Eden dwelt, and were the angels' care.

" Then slowly dawn'd on my awaken'd mind
 Remembrance how that garden, earth and sky,
Shone bright in darkness to the Poet blind,
 Forming the world none save himself could spy.
So grew within me yearning to console
 That lonely sufferer in his blighted age,—
To speak the rapture rising in my soul,
 Born of his harmony and sacred page.

" When the first snow had fallen, I saw him stand
    With a bewilder'd air, almost of dread,
  As one who wander'd in an unknown land,
    And knew not, amid perils, where to tread.
  Then, ere I weigh'd my rashness, my words came ;
    And like a king accepting proffer'd dues
  From loyal hearts, without distrust or shame,
    Guidance and love he could not well refuse.

" That day began new life in me, he learn'd
    All I had long'd to say, and press'd my hand :
  Thus for my vigils best reward I earn'd,
    And can the poet's heart now understand.
  What do I heed that ignorance decries
    The inspiration, and repeats old blame?
  I mourn his erroneous ' Tractates ' ; but I prize
    The unsullied genius that attains true Fame."

The Westminster-Drolleries.

(Choicest of Cavalier Song-books, from 1671 *to* 1674.*)*

If ye be weary of the drowsy hum
    Of silly Senators and Legal folly,
The boasts of 'Scientists' (all wrangling), come,
    These *Drolleries* free you soon from melancholy.
A pleasant hour you'll spend with Cavaliers,
    Their roystering fun, their catches and cajolery,
Their love-lays—with more smiles than trace of tears ;
    The varied phases of *Westminster-Drollery.*

Shadows before us move of buried Wits,
    Beau Sedley, Dorset, CHARLES with frank good nature ;
Once more, at Will's, enthroned, John Dryden sits,
    Twitting friend Davenant on nasal feature.
Wilmot and Aphra Behn strike amorous strings,
    Tom Brown, Hicks, D'Urfey, joining in the chorus ;
Wycherley lends fresh mirth, plump Shadwell sings,
    Starched Johnny Crowne perks his grave phiz before us.

Playwrights and Poets, not unknown to fame,
    With mockery of Wife, or ode to Spinster,
Gibing at Puritan and Roundhead, came
    Entwining *Drolleries* from old *Westminster* :
Garlands unfaded, theirs, with perfume still,
    For all who hold Stuart White Rose in favour, -
All who can quaff the true Castalian rill,
    And like it better for its antique flavour.

On the Pantiles at Tonbridge-Wells.

(Where the Court took the Waters, circâ 1675.)

" I grow weary, my Chloe, of raptures and darts,
All the silly romance of exchanging our hearts;
Since I find that your beauty is vanishing fast,
Let me seek a new pleasure, more likely to last.
    Having laid costly gifts on a false goddess' shrine,
    I leave Woman, the fickle, and now worship Wine.

" I see plainly that Chloe indignant is shock'd,
Having heard my confession, and known herself mock'd;
No woman is pleas'd to be left in the lurch,
For a rival or flaggon, at tavern or church:
    But if only the nymph had proved loving and kind,
    I (perhaps) had not whistled her now down the wind.

" You rejoin, on behalf of Fair Chloe, that I
Am myself not so bright, since my Spring-time went by?
Well, admitting thus much, as to figure and bloom,
Wisdom comes with *bonnes Fortunes*; Wit conquers gloom,
    I can laugh at most evils that threaten man's life;
    But, by Bacchus! none laughs if a shrew be his wife."

Lauderdale's Black 'Bess.'

(Her portrait after Sir Peter Lely, 1677.)

" Whom Burnet hates must need have some points good :
    Carrion he scents, in all deem'd pure or sweet !
Greedy for flattery, as a hen for food,
    The truckling priest is choak-full of conceit.
Bess proves no Lucrece—that is understood—
    But she treads ' lying Gibbie ' 'neath her feet :
Since the revengeful Scots in spite long brood,
    He'll doubly-dye her ' Black,' when his *Own Time's* complete."

The Canon of Christ-Church.

(Islip Rectory, Oxon., 1678.)

Who would not cringe, or back-stairs tread,
And be by courtly minions led
To cloak their sins, must need have said
        ' Nolo Episcopari !'

Who, when the Monarch dozed, could preach
As calmly, and true virtue teach,
Hoping more tender hearts to reach :
        ' Nolo episcopari.'

Who sought no luxury and pride,
But left the sycophants to ride,
While he knelt at the poor's bedside :
        ' Nolo episcopari.'

Who held aloof from plots and schemes,
And never quail'd at Faction's screams,
Or mourn'd th' awakening from dreams :
        ' Nolo episcopari.'

Who the pure Gospel loved so well
That rapturously his heart would swell ;
Thence chose in lowlier seat to dwell :
        ' Nolo episcopari.'

Who, prizing learned leisure rare,
And all the privilege of prayer,
Shrank from the hireling Prelate's fare :
        ' Nolo episcopari.'

Who, loathing Judas' bribes, and drouth
Of Tantalus' ever-gaping mouth,
Still stood upright, plain **Robert South** :
        ' Nolo episcopari !'

H

The Ballad-Singer of Stuart Days.

(*London Wall, September* 13, '78.)

"Come around me, ye bountiful Masters,
    My ballads and songs, pray, now hear!
I laid in a fresh stock of Disasters,
    To make you all shudder with fear.
I could curdle your blood, with a many;
    Or make your flesh creep, with a few;
I might shock you to death for one penny:
    And warrant the whole of them true.

"But I know you need change from such diet,
    (Since variety suits you and me);
You shall have, if you only be quiet,
    No more Battles, on land or at Sea,
But as much Love and Mirth, for your money,
    As a Cavalier Hector e'er knew:
Till around you the world become sunny,
    And you fancy it all made for you.

"Far away from your present small troubles
    To the Past of these ballads return:
There are gay hues, methinks, on their bubbles,
    Bright sparks amid embers yet burn.
Let the cynic growl, 'Soap-suds! all hollow;'
    Or the saint mutter, 'Brands for the flame!'
Street-songs were not scorn'd by Apollo—
    So I offer them now, in his name."

J. W. E.

(Ballad-Singer of Stuart Days: after Inigo Jones.)

" Come, buy my Ballads, broadside-ballads, buy !
    Lovers who willow wore, and maids betray'd,
Herein could find congenial sympathy,
    And we who sold them briskly drove our trade.
Tear-drops have fallen on these wither'd leaves,
    Roysters have sung blithe strains from ditties here :
Who will, may choose the Hanging-verse of Thieves;
    Who will, the Storm-song of bold Marinere."

Nellie.

(Episcopus Anglicanus loquitur. Diœcesis Ignota, 1678.)

" Let the crop-ear'd Roundheads loathe and hate !
We care not a rush for their canting prate,
Though nothing they praise in Church or State,
    So why should I complain ?—
If they talk for a year, with snivel and whine,
Of the ' black disgrace and accurst decline
That befel an orthodox Court divine,'
    Seeking Nellie in Drury-Lane.

" It was early morn in the month of June,
My heart with the season felt in tune ;
I had studied late, and risen soon,
    Little of sleep I had ta'en :
I knew that a ramble might do me good,
Through Convent-Garden, to cool my blood,
So I gather'd a rose, pass'd on, and stood
    Beside Nellie in Drury-Lane.

" She had slipt down stairs to fetch her milk,
In her short smock sleeves, with skin like silk,
When Scotch laird Lauriston o' that Ilk
  ' To speak wi' the Lass ' was fain ;
But she gave him his answer, while I drew near,
Her silvery laugh sounding fresh and clear :
Little our pretty Nell Gwynne need fear,
  Though she dwells in Drury-Lane.

" She's the brightest of beauties, by all confest,
She can flaunt as a tragedy-queen with the best,
Or with rollicking Hectors break a jest,
  For a giddy hour or twain ;
They say that an oath will not make her start :
But this I well know, for my honest part,
In London-town beats no warmer heart
  Than Nellie's of Drury-Lane.

" I had seen her first as an Orange-girl
At the theatre door, with her saucy curl,
She soon set the gallants' heads in a whirl,
  Then began her actress reign ;
For both Davenant and Tom Killigrew
Bade high for her presence, when they knew
That her face a crowd of admirers drew
  Around her in Drury-Lane.

" Why even our King (I have heard them say)
Found Affairs of State must brook delay
When Nellie had some new part to play,
             In a hat like wheel of wain ;
So, mayhap—though a mitre 'twould have cost—
I'd have counted for her the world well lost,
Had ' Old Rowley' himself my path not crost
             When I sought her, in Drury-Lane.

" I once might have won her, with a word,
When my heart with a glance of her eye was stirr'd,
Though my Patron had voted the match absurd,
             And left me my bread to gain.
Yet I oft-times sigh at the drearier life
Of sermon and homily, sects and strife,
I have sunk to, instead of the winsom wife
             Whom I found not, in Drury-Lane."

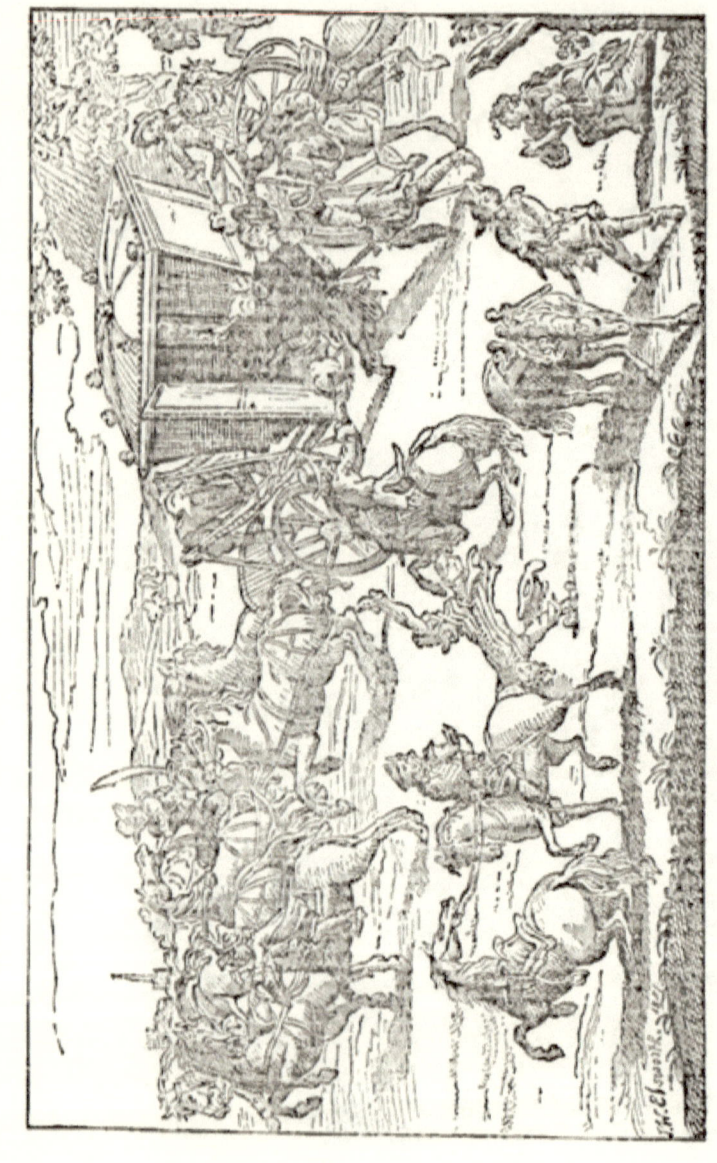

MURDER OF ARCHBISHOP SHARP, BY THE SCOTTISH COVENANTERS, ON MAGUS MUIR, 1679.

When Archbishop Sharp was Murdered.

(Magus-Moor, Fifeshire, May 3, 1679.)

" Between the thunderbolts of Papal pride
　And more envenom'd stabs of Calvin's gang,
Who boast their 'Covenant,' let choice decide :
　Intolerant hatred gnaws with deadlier fang.
Since Magus-moor Scotch prelate's blood has dyed,
　While shouts of 'curst apostate !' dirge-like rang,
We in the South, by Rome's plots terrified,
　Cry—'Plague on both your houses !' Head or hang ! "

The Watcher at Whitehall.

(Tempo Caroli Secundi, circâ 1679.)

They kept not well their watch and ward,
　But left Whitehall unclosed to me,
While I slipt softly past the Guard,
　And roved through every chamber free.

The Pages yawn'd, though 'twas high noon,
　Some half-asleep lean'd near the Throne;
Unawed, lest Charles might enter soon,
　And mock them in his light gay tone.

They heeded not, or idly stared,
　But scandal lisp'd in languid drawl;
While on through mirror'd rooms I fared,
　Leaving in haste the Banquet-Hall.　　[*In Mem*
　　　　　　　　　　　　　　　　　　　　　　y Jan.

Pictures of Saints and Nymphs on high,
　Brocades flung loose across the screens;
Here "Madam Carwell's" haunts I spy,
　Tenfold more gorgeous than the Queen's.

Lap-dogs sleep cushion'd near the fire,
　A crucifix, gold chain, and pearls,
A French Romance, half froth, half mire,
　Lie heap'd, with harp-strings and false curls.

Ye Gods! who holds yon sleeping room ?
    What faëry-land retreat I see !
Faint with comminglings of perfume ;
    Hush'd from all sounds of revelry.

Not tenantless, when I draw near
    To cross the threshold, half in dread :
I see her laughing face appear,
    With rosy flush, from out the bed.

Swift through the corridor I grope,
    An open door admits me then
Into the chamber of my hope :
    It is—" OLD ROWLEY'S " secret den !

Here crucibles, retorts, and flasks,
    Gossamer threads of poisèd scales,
Tell of the questions Science asks,
    And tell how oft the answer fails.

For here Projection has been tried,
    Gold wasted, but no gold return'd ;
The flame long fed, that luckless died :
    The midnight oil, that useless burn'd.

Here too are skeletons, all blanch'd,
    Jointed with springs of rarest skill ;
Models of ships that ne'er were launch'd :
    Vials, with drugs to cure or kill.

Tired of Earth's follies, crimes, and wars,
  Hither our King was wont to pass,
And, girt by all these charts of stars,
  Peer through this mounted object-glass.

Free, for the hour, from wanton wiles
  Of gipsies, whom none else could trust;
Free from the magic of their smiles,
  Their boundless greed, their saucy " Must ! "—

Here, in the silence of the night,
  He heard some better voices call;
Won glimpse of Heaven's diviner light,
  And reign'd sole Watcher in Whitehall.

E.

Lesson of the Sham Popish-Plot.

(Anti-Papal phrensy of '41 revived, 1680.)

We do not urge, " Because our times are evil,
  Look back upon these records of old years !"*
We stir no feud 'twixt Commoners and Peers ;
But hate your grievance-monger like a weevil.
  Our plea is this : " Since in the Past were errors
Like to our own, with noise and bitter vaunts,
Proclaim'd by Sectaries, self-styled ' Protestants,'
  They warn true men to hold in scorn their terrors."
See, in the Rebels of the *Good Old Cause,*
  By whom the tares of mischief had been sown,
The ante-types of men who now hate Laws !
  One crop the first Charles reap'd, another's grown,
Poisonous, threat'ning Church and Crown: Why pause ?
  Beware delay of sickles ! Mow it down !

* Vide *Roxburghe Ballads*, Second Series, 1881 to 1887.

With Will Longueville, the Friend of 'Hudibras.'

(*From his Temple-chambers to Butler's bedside in Rose-Street, Covent-Garden, September 25, 1680.*)

"Why do you glare at me so strangely, Will?
　Is it a ghost that you have seen to-night?
Art rous'd from sleep by shrieks, or dreaming still?
　Can you not speak, and bid me share your fright?
Nay, man! I know your courage: none so well
　As I, your true companion of old days;
And, while I talk with you, there seem to swell
　Within my heart sweet anthems to your praise.

"Say, what has wrought this havoc of your peace?—
　You, who are always temperate and grave,
Shrewd in your business, knowing no surcease
　Of legal toil, although spent nature crave:
Good son and faithful friend, past all who live;
　Stainless defender of each virtuous cause;
Who, eloquently standing forth, dost give
　To the oppress'd the ægis of just laws.

" It cannot be, because I jest and droll
 When gay companions meet around your board,
And take my share in emptying the bowl,
 That you can doubt my fullness of accord ?
If sorrow come to shock you, let me share
 Whatever burden on your heart be laid :
If wealth is perill'd, small has been your care
 To gather dross like hirelings whelp'd in trade.

" So, now you find your tongue, and tell your grief,
 I too can feel your shuddering chill and fear :
Yet have we had forewarnings, half-belief,
 Seeing him daily change, that Death draws near.
Let me go with you to the lowly bed,
 Where rests the brightest genius of our age ;
Let me once more—before his soul has fled—
 Clasp his worn hand, our satirist and sage.

" How solemnly we feel the stilly night,
 Here in our Temple-chambers, where we dwell !
Only in yon high casement gleams a light,
 Showing some student thrall'd by Themis' spell,
Hark ! to the fountain's trickling tinkling chime,
 Between the echoes of our halting feet :—
Thus have I heard its music many a time,
 In my so lonely life, and deem'd it sweet.

"Plague on the drowsy Porter! will he not
    Answer our summons and unlock the gate ?—
Forgive my wrath, impatient, I forgot—
    The churl is deaf who forces us to wait.
There, now we are free, and through the silent street
    Move on our way, hush'd like the busy town :
Had I kept mute perchance it were more meet,
    But that I dread my thought, and crush it down.

"One! Two! no later?—we are in time, belike.
    The ghastly 'Three of morn' I dread the most
Of all the hours that after midnight strike,
    For then our vital strength seems almost lost ;
The lamp burns dimly, sinks the smouldering fire,
    The blood turns cold, and a vague terror falls
On those who tend sick-beds, with omens dire :
    Ticks a death-watch, strange shadows haunt the walls.

"How would he mock such idle fear, whose gibes
    Smote astrologic science, hip and thigh !
Yet held he sympathy with mystic tribes,
    Versed in Cabala, and the doctrines high
Of Rosicrucian lore, and Talmud page ;
    Quaint hieroglyphics, and the airiest dreams
Of early Platonists or Gnostics sage :
    All the bright fancies wherewith darkness teems.

" He was no puling Poet, drunk with rhymes
    Of soft conceit, Love's ecstasy and woe ;
But one whose heartfelt interest in our times
    And loyal fervour all the world doth know.
Beneath his lash Hypocrisy might howl
    And gnash the teeth, or mutter vengeance dire ;
While rank Rebellion paid with spite and scowl
    The scornful notes of his Satyric lyre.

" How have we revell'd in that humour bright,
    Flashing undimm'd through each successive page !
We laugh'd o'er tales of the Quixotic wight
    Who squired by Ralpho did fierce crowds engage.
We saw the knight in combat overthrown,
    Bestrid by Trulla or in stocks encased ;
We heard each sanctimonious Brother groan;
    When to the conclave frighted posts would haste.

" Who like our Butler legal quibbles knew,
    Petty chicanery and precedent ?—
Who so well scourged the Presbyterian crew,
    Or probed the windbag of Rump-Parliament ?
Others had suffered from oppression long
    The pains and penalties for loyal deeds;
None could like him translate their woes to song,
    And raise a mirthful smile from bitterest needs.

I

" He, the lone Student, doom'd to toils obscure—
    For whom no firelight gleam'd, no loving eyes
Of wife or child long welcom'd, pain to cure,
    Or win to hopefulness and glad surprise—
Uncounted among Powers of the State,
    As friend or foe, hence left in covert sure:
Now, at the close of life, acknowledged great,
    Above all despots, of true fame secure.

" Fame? lo, our squalid Rose-street, where he dwells!
    Where not a year ago ruffians waylaid
And nearly murder'd Dryden (so he tells),   [*Dec. 18, 1679.*
    Cudgell'd for what sleek Mulgrave wrote or said;
Here Butler ' Hudibras ' might rot and die,
    Unheeded by the courtly men of Taste:
He would have starved, had you, Will, pass'd him by,
    Leaving the nation by his death disgraced.

" His door stands open, ' Thieves break through and steal '
    Nothing from such a house, in such a street.
But hush! he rests in slumber; let us kneel,
    Thankful that he still breathes, for life is sweet.
How calm, how worn he looks! patient and mild,
    Hollow in cheek, of old so round and red,
Now pale and ghastly: hours had he beguil'd
    With wit and wisdom that too fleetly sped.

" Never again, Oh ! never, shall we hear
    His wondrous knowledge clothed in choicest words ;
Epigrammatic now, terse and severe ;
    Then fluent, carolling like the song of birds :
Full of old-world allusions, while he drew
    On some chance scrap those portraits Cooper prized :
Reserv'd with strangers, ever by the few
    Who met him frankly, loved and idolized.

" Yes, you were right ! the last change has began ;
    Feeble the pulse, the breath more labour'd now :
And this is all remaining of the man
    Who mirror'd human nature in his brow.
So high in dignity of soul, so true,
    Loyal and gentle, that we almost mourn
His wasted powers, on works the world can view,
    While noblest thoughts within him die unborn.

" For you, Will Longueville, his opening-eyes
    Are seeking wistfully ; and now you bend
Across his pillow, while he feebly tries
    To his parched lips to raise your hand : '*My friend!*'
Hear his eternal blazon of your name,
    His own true friend ! loved till his latest breath.
Idle at best is all our world-wide fame :—
    He smiles, he blesses you.   And this is death."

In Alsatia, after Nightfall.

(Whitefriars, during the Sham 'Popish-Plot' phrenzy, October, 1680.)

" Rollicking Boys, in debt or in drink,
   Filchers, who grabble at other folks' chink,
   Lightskirts, unwilling to beat hemp or swink,
        Come away here to Alsatia !
   Nobody asks you for licence or leave ;
   Tell truth or lies, not a soul you deceive ;
   Hang, drown, or stab yourselves, little we grieve :
        No one is miss'd in Alsatia.

" Flaunt you by day, or slink hither by night,
   Squalid your duds, or in flash rigging dight,
   Pay but your garnish, then lodgement comes right :
        No question asked in Alsatia.
   ' Gentlemen's honour respect we so much ! '
   All join to baffle the Tipstaff's rude clutch ;
   Rash fool were he, who with writ dare to touch
        Black-Will in Mint or Alsatia.

" Noisy our taverns, foul-gutter'd our lanes,
 Frouzy our rooms, dim and shatter'd our panes,
  ' Landlords must live ! '—knaves pocket big gains :
            Dog feeds on dog in Alsatia.
 Best not to murmur, pride goes before fall ;
 Keep with discretion outside of a brawl :
 Heads are soon broken when Tat-mongers call
            ' Bailiff'—' Arrest '—in Alsatia.

" Lost are distinctions, like virtue and fears ;
 Beggars or borrowers, commons or peers,
 Sulky old Roundheads or putt Cavaliers,
            Find their snug holes in Alsatia :
 Zealot ' Fifth-Monarchists,' quick-set to stab ;
 Swash-bucklers, trading with dice and with drab ;
 Knights-of-the-Post, who forswear and then blab :
            Room for them all in Alsatia.

" Cave of Adullam (so we used to read,
 In a book little prized save for neck-verse at need,)
 Our prototype was, but its fame we exceed
            In privileged den of Alsatia :
 Whatever our cause be of new discontent,
 If hunted by ' stags,' or on mischief bent,
 Only a sleuth-hound of keenest scent
            Could track us to earth in Alsatia.

" Dark ways lead into it, worse ways lead out ;
The river flows pleasantly near us, no doubt,
Convenient to catch any slippery trout
    Who sniffs at stale bait in Alsatia ;
Since Dangerfield, Bedloe, and Titus Oates
(Changing their creeds, when they turn'd their coats),
With halter and axe now threaten our throats,
    No place is safe but Alsatia.

" Where mingle morts, cullies, and apple-squires,
Britons of old crouch'd around marsh-fires,
Displaced in good time by jolly White-Friars :
    Sanctified land ! now Alsatia.
Loyal community, best left alone ;
Works a brisk trade, having laws of its own :
Safer from Plotters than Charles on his throne,
    Broken men thrive in Alsatia.

F.

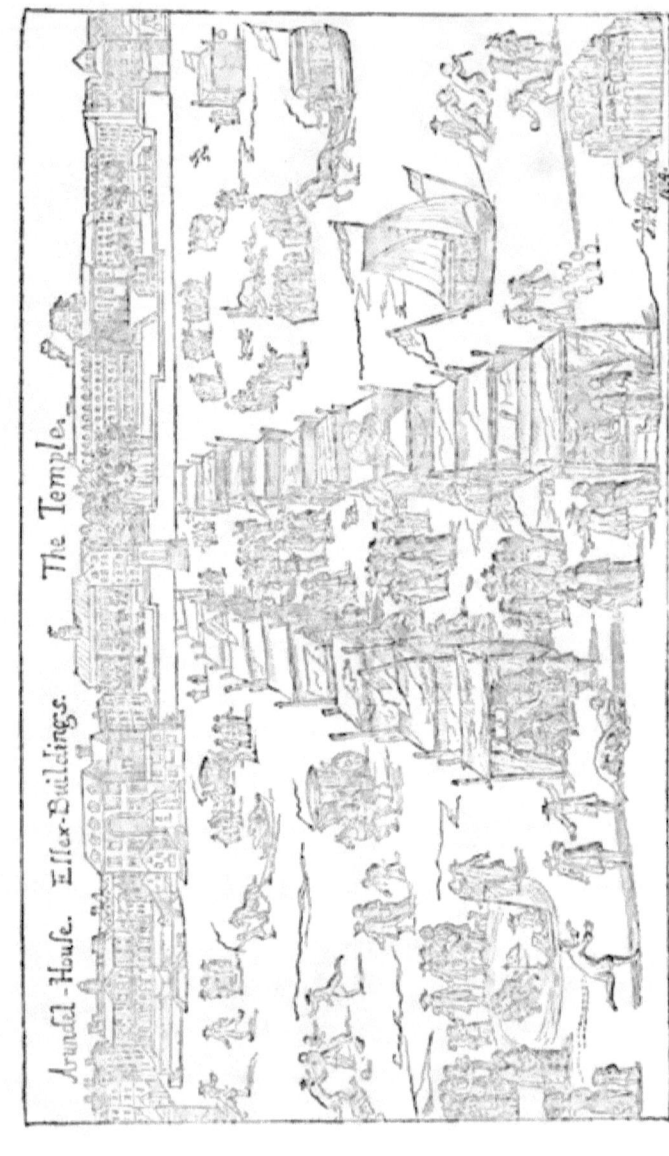

Arundel-House.   Effex-Buildings.   The Temple.

FROST-FAIR, ON THE RIVER THAMES, IN 1683-84.

(From a Contemporary Engraving.)

London, in Autumn.

(September, 1683.)

" My thoughts oft flit to you in rhythmic measure,
 Without an effort, as a rose breathes scent ;
Simply because to dream of you is pleasure,
 And in my heart still dwells a sweet content ;
You too remember it, that hill-top shady,
 The golden sunset, with the river near ?—
I saw the irradiate beauty of ' My Ladie ' :
 You saw the glade, and your own Cavalier."

London, in Winter.

(Frost-Fair, February, 168¾.)

" Come, join their sport ! our river Thames is frozen ;
 See ! where our barge had floated, coaches roll ;
Gay citizens now troop in cloaks and hosen ;
 O'er blazing faggots roast they oxen whole ;
Through streets of canvas booths from Temple-garden
 Across the ice to Southwark shore we go :
No frost can chill thy warm young heart, or harden,
 Though my dark locks may soon be fleck'd with snow."

A Gossip at Deptford.

(On Samuel Pepys, Replaced Secretary to the Admiralty, 1684.)

"Do you wonder I like him, the best of all men?
    Though I grant he is heavy and solemn and dull,
When you meet him at Council, with word or pen:
    You don't know half the wisdom stored in his skull.
Not half? not a tithe! He's no idler at work,
    The State has no servant in all whom she keeps
Like my squab little friend, who no labour does shirk,
    The pattern of quill-driving clerks, Sam Pepys.

"Do you know what a pack he has had to controul?—
    Peculators and sneaks, downright liars and thieves,
Men born into the world with no scrap of a soul,
    Men whose solemn oath never a street drab believes.
With colleagues who truckle, take bribes from the French,
    Smile blandly at thought of the vengeance that sleeps;
Who pass jests on Charles when they toy with his wench;
    Is there one who can boast of alliance with Pepys?

" To his duty he's true, and wherever he sees
    The Navy despoil'd, he speaks out like a man ;
He knows well the risk, and he dearly loves ease,
    But temptation of pleasure ne'er alters his plan.
Our seamen's complaints find him urgent to aid ;
    If timber is stolen or rotting in heaps,
Or the honour of England seems nearly betray'd,
    Up starts to the rescue undaunted Sam Pepys.

" In the dockyards they know his true worth, and a cheer
    Would rise from each shed-full of men, be you sure,
Were not discipline strict ; but he cares not to hear
    From shipwrights what conscience must echo secure.
Yet he makes no pretence to be hero or saint,
    With the joyous he laughs, with mourners he weeps ;
He's not one who at bilge-water turns pale and faint,
    But a man with sound courage and skill is Sam Pepys.

" He was something of Puritan once, in Nol's time,
    And perhaps pious phrases drop from him too oft ;
But Religion we need not count wholly a crime,
    Though we find little piety now up aloft.
Some snigger and sniff at his proneness to prayers,
    And the ' liking for books and such lumber he sweeps ;'
While others are shock'd at his fondness for Players :
    The girls in the 'tiring-room worship Sam Pepys.

"You should hear him, at home, when his viol's in tune,
  Or his voice joins in harmony dulcet and true,
 Take my word, you would hardly be one to leave soon,
  Though his wife (looking jealous of Knipp) is a shrew.
 To male-gossips he listens; when wanton eyes gaze
  From maid, wife, or widow, his heart bounds and leaps:
 I saw him kiss Nelly, who acted stage-plays,
  And she kiss'd him back again. O! Mistress Pepys!

"Now, you see, we who know him have made up our mind
  Not to heed the vile slanders of pamphleteers' mob,
 But to stand up for one who is honest and kind,
  And will suffer no traitors to ruin or rob.
 So they call him 'a Papist,' because he loves James,
  High-Admiral York, ruling barques on our deeps;
 But no Papist is he, who keeps watch on the Thames,
  Over Ship-yard at Deptford, my old friend Sam Pepys.

Trifling with Love.

"Assured that my Eros a Rose always bore,
  I twisted my Eros, until he felt Sore:
 He was *Eros reversus*, the wrong end before.

"When again I tried Amor, the truant, to bind,
  He led me to Roma, fresh puzzle to find:
 As Maro and Omar well knew ' Love is blind!' "

[*One of Sam Pepys' ducklings: reduced copy of a contemporary woodcut*, a " Sovereign of the Seas " line of battle ship, time of Charles II.]

Uncompanioned.

In the Land of the bright Hereafter,
   Whither I glide away,
Shall I hear the mocking laughter
   Of the spirit that used to say,
"Oh thou, who in proud seclusion
   Unhoping, uncheer'd, hast dwelt,
Not blinded by fools' delusion,
   Not humbled where converts knelt,

"Can'st thou hold a share in rapture,
   After mourning so long thy loss ?—
Can'st thou hope any Crown to capture,
   Who hast murmur'd beneath thy Cross ?"
While it echoes, not this time only,
   But as oft in the bygone years,
I shall mutely smile, and pass lonely
   Wherever my path appears.

Ballads of the Seventeenth Century.

Come, buy my ballads, Harley's Ballads, buy!
　　Black-letter broadsides, saved from Father Time;
Full of rude cuts, but ripe for History,
　　That oft finds nourishment in rabble-rhyme.
He who would trace the ages pass'd away,
　　And see old English homesteads round him rise,
Fill'd with the men and women of their day,
　　Must list these echoes of their melodies.

Come, buy my ballads, Bodleian Ballads, come!
　　And read betwixt the lines what grief and pain
Were borne of old, while beat the martial drum,
　　And Ladies wept for those in battle slain.
Rolls o'er the billows many a sound of fight,
　　Scorn of the foe, and shout of victory;
Changed to the Sailor's welcome in delight,
　　When home again to sweetheart, safe from sea.

Come, buy my ballads, Pepysian Ballads, buy!
　　Lovers who willow wore, and maids betray'd,
Herein could find congenial sympathy,
　　Albeit the rhymester ply'd a sorry trade.
Tear-drops have fallen on these wither'd leaves,
　　Roysters have sang blithe staves from others here:
Who will, may choose the Hanging-verse of Thieves;
　　Who will, the Storm-song of bold Marinere.

Ave, Caesar! morituri te salutant.

(A Tribute to the Manes of Carolus Secundus, Feb., 168⅖.)

I saw in a Vision, through tremulous light,
    On the borders Elysian of Hades,
Our Cavaliers gathered: priest, noble, and knight,
    Civic magnates, court poets, and Ladies.

Each face I knew well, some bewitchingly fair,
    Though at times too self-conscious or haughty,
Yet for once their bright lustre was shadow'd by care:
    Others, bold and defiant, look'd naughty.

The gayest of revellers now could not speak
    Trim compliments, jibes, and wit-flashes;
A chill from the Death-stream had whiten'd our cheek:
    True tears of grief hung on eye-lashes.

Each wore a black mantle, black scarf, plume and gloves,
    So intensely bereavement we reckon'd;
Even Venus had changed into ravens her doves:
    For we mourn'd our lost King, Charles the Second.

"The longer we knew him," the chief of us cried,
    "The better we loved and approved him;
We had rather have seen that all common folks died,
    Than that Death so unkindly removed him.

" Some people dare say he had faults!" [*cries of 'Shame!'*]
 " They hint about bribes from King Lewis ! !
 Also women" ['*a few!*'], "not unsmirch'd in fair fame !!!
 Were such small errors reckon'd, we knew his.

" A Spendthrift, perhaps, but no Miser was he,
 To hoard up the nation's grudged riches ;
 He loved others to please, and be pleased, frank and free,
 While he sported with ducklings, and——spaniels !

" A man of the world, with sound hatred of Cant,
 And a habit of 'making things pleasant,'
 He had smiled at the 'Saintly's' fanatical rant,
 That did mischief to townsfolk and peasant.

" In a land wreck'd by schism and rebellion, like ours,
 When from Exile return'd, welcom'd gladly,
 What King could 'scape error, so crippled in powers,
 After youth spoilt in wandering sadly ?

" No tyrant was he, would they leave him in peace ;
 He was kind to his children and brother ;
 When life lost its zest, he found happy release :
 Long 'twill be ere we see such Another !"

Here we all shed our tears, laid a wreath on his tomb,
 So departed, with sobbing and sorrow ;
 Gave the rest of the night-time to sermons and gloom,
 Then—paid court to King James on the morrow.

"King Monmouth," 1685.

(*L'Envoi to the Roxburghe Ballads, of his Life and Times.*)

To the Tune of, *Captain Radcliffe's Ramble.*

Two centuries have pass'd away
Since poor 'King Monmouth' turn'd to clay,
And little more is left to say
      About him.
His hapless fate moves not our tears,
But, since we trace from earliest years
His hopes, his follies, faults and fears,
      Don't flout him !

Poor pageant-puppet, whom the crowd
Worship'd with clamour long and loud !
No wonder his weak head grew proud,
      And tumbled ;
Such time as with 'religious cries'
Mock-patriots forged conspiracies,
And, spite of their intrigues and lies,
      Were humbled.

True students mark the records here
Of what men thought in earlier year;
Th' Handwriting on the Wall shines clear
          With warning;
To our mind, there is nothing lost
If we, who count the former cost,
Beware like errors: men err most
          By scorning.

Two centuries ago! and still
The frauds of old remain to kill;
Each mis-directed human will
          Brings peril;
In hatred Schismatists divide,
As when the mob 'No Popery' cried:
Their folly welters like a tide,
          But sterile.

Then call not 'Ballads out of date'
These poems on affairs of State;
Some are of Courtiers' love or hate,
          Some lowly;
They show us—if we be not blind—
Whirlwinds are reap'd where men sow'd wind:
Whether the plotting Whigs or kind
          "Old Rowley!"

After a Score of Years.

(Esher, July 6, 1686.)

Count them not lost, the years I gave
To her, whom still my soul doth crave,
　　And craves for ever ;
Though in the world I find her not,
Seeking her, heart-sick, in each spot,
　　With vain endeavour.

They were not lost.　No fen-fire ray
Led me through devious paths astray ;
　　Her light was holy !
No other gleam so sweetly cheer'd,
As that which from the first appear'd
　　Meant for me solely.

'Twas worth the cost : full well we knew,
Who early loved, hearts tried and true,
　　What Life's best bliss is ;
Such as outweigh'd these griefs to come,
Prepayment for all future gloom :—
　　One of her kisses.

Whispered.

(In Memoriam M. L.)

I think that the saddest of human cares
　　That on earth we are doom'd to know
Is remembrance of all the blessings and prayers
　　Laid on us, so long ago !—
By those who have died and gone away
　　With their love for us unrepaid ;
Who can never hear what we now would say,
　　But had left in the past unsaid.

Our tears vainly fall, in remorse, too late ;
　　Dead flowers on the friend beloved ;
Till despair turn to hope that Beyond the Gate
　　Our truth may at last be proved ;
For here bewilder'd we lost our way,
　　We fail'd in our life-long quest ;
We await, and shall find, the brighter Day :
　　Patience and Trust are best.

With John Evelyn at Sayes Court, 1687.

"And so the Meeting pass'd off well, you say.
    Laid up with this sciatica, half-blind,
An owl, and no sun-gazing bird of day,
    I love to hear what you to tell are kind.
Well, thus the world advances with vast strides ;
    How wise men grow, since you and I were young !
Science now draws to light what Nature hides,
    And Newton speaks results with reverent tongue.

" Glad should I be, could I adventure forth
    Like you, John Evelyn ; meet the friends you meet ;
I who have spent long nights with Roger North,
    Revell'd with Scroggs and Jeffereys, hard to beat.
Yet have I risen triumphant, seen both down,
    Under the table prone, myself unharm'd.
Well, well, those days are past, so do not frown,
    And then look shock'd.   See, my life was not charm'd !

" I think you travell'd, all those tragic years
    While civil-wars raged here, and Commonwealth
Laid heavier chains on us than our new seers
    Can make allowance for.   Men spoke by stealth,
Treachery hem'd them round, malicious spies,
    Quick to report such words as no man spoke ;
Most piercing through the dark were envious eyes,
    Foreseeing evil—told ere morning broke.

" Few were the scholars who lived through that time
    Without disguise of name and change of place,
Faintest suspected loyalty was crime ;
    Unstain'd religious faith was black disgrace.
Old-promis'd liberty was out of date :
    The worst of slavery for heart and soul
Was laid on us, who dwelt outside the gate
    Where flush'd Rebellion bribed with proffer'd dole.

" Those wasted years ! no Temple student throve
    Who could not favour win from some grim ' saint ' ;
Discountenanc'd, he might as well go rove
    Through alien lands, and swell the loud complaint.
True Learning was in beggary : our fanes
    Of sacred knowledge, Cam and Isis both,
Were desecrated, plunder'd, with blood stains
    On many a house, miscall'd ' of Pride and Sloth.'

" You knew my brother.   His the lore divine
    That lifts man nighest heaven : so small his need
He had resign'd his birthright, made it mine,
    Hoping to see me in high walks succeed.
No holier life than his, no sweeter voice
    Told of God's ways to man, led man to God ;
Such pastor as should be a people's choice,
    If wisdom ruled them in the path they trod.

" He was no bigot ; he had griev'd when Laud
    Enforced some harsh decrees of earlier day ;
But he was faithful, and thus dared to applaud
    That master's worth, while in the Tower he lay.
Such could not be forgiven, so word was sent
    To drive him from his fold, to wrench his crook
From the good shepherd's hand, who, well content,
    Despoil'd of home, not yet his flock forsook.

" Harsh, brutal were our rebel tyrants all.
    Those who befriended him were dragg'd to jail,
Fined, branded, scourged : Hunted from hut and stall,
    Famish'd and chill'd, his strength erelong might fail.
But courage triumph'd over foes' despite ;
    Confessor, almost martyr, he laid down
All that the world holds dear, seeking true Light ;
    And his last words were still, ' No Cross, no Crown!'

" Mine then were devious paths, apart from him ;
    Perils no less, not with like patience borne ;
My young life shatter'd, future looming dim,
    I paid back hate for hate, and scorn for scorn.
Obscure, as humble tutor, I found rest ;
    Or plied the pen as clerk to Justice dull ;
Flashing abroad by stealth the biting jest,
    Which could not penetrate my patron's skull.

"Gladly I learnt (almost my only pride)
     Street-ballads I had writ' proclaim'd and bann'd ;
Lampoons on 'Zion's Wiseacres' decried ;
     Thenceforward sought with zest throughout the land.
Bitter my laugh, when Searchers would take note,
     'Tryers,' to track my secret, questioning school ;
Contemning my soil'd linen, threadbare coat,
     And hollow cheek : I foil'd them, shamming 'fool.'

"Still in lone hours I studied books of Law,
     Liv'd spare, perforce, shun'd drink lest tongue might blab,
Practis'd the wiles that keep from reach of claw
     Alike the satirist and men who stab.
Some secret commerce with mark'd knaves I held,
     (Such times admitted no nice rules of choice,)
Till Cromwell's death the doom of faction knell'd :
     'Welcome, King Charles !' out-spoke the people's voice.

"Then safety came to me, and favour too ;
     At once I found flowers strewn upon my path ;
Legal distinction open'd to my view ;
     My wit hail'd now, that once had waken'd wrath.
Sour'd by long years of unrequited toil,
     Scarcely subservient as the time might need,
But subtle, accurate, thanks to midnight oil :
     Brow-beater, not brow-beaten, must succeed.

" Hard won, each sure advance, you have seen me rise,
    Not quite approving, yet not harsh in blame ;
Until supreme as Judge I won the prize :
    Nor was my conscience wrong'd by deed of shame.
Loyal, I held ' Dispensing Kingly-Power '
    Incontrovertible, on ground secure :
Pliant in this, I suited well my hour,
    But kept my hand unsoil'd from bribe impure.

" Already crippled, forced to private life,
    My spirit feels no freshen'd hope return ;
In you, who held your course remov'd from strife,
    I see the pure white flame serenely burn.
You mingle, welcom'd, loved, with learned men,
    Who in Society of Royal stamp
Bring wondrous Science to our startled ken ;
    Patiently trimming still the mystic lamp.

" *Et ego in Arcadiâ vixi !*   Gone
    The unsullied hope that first my heart inspired ;
Regretfully I gaze that Past upon :
    See chill dead ashes where the flame then fired.
Ah, friend ! whose life through gentler channels flow'd,
    Pass no stern judgement on my turbid stream !
Clasp hands once more, where calmly you abode :
    Sorrow and joy we shared : Each dreamt his dream."

Semper Fidelis.

(Gravesend, December 18, 1688.)

"So then, he flings up cards: King James has fled!
  Nothing remains for us to do on shore.
Sad were his parting words, that no hope fed—
  No faintest hope of his return once more.
Vainly we urged him, 'Stay, and face the worst!
  From trickster Orange and those pliant knaves
Whom he had bribed to treachery accurst:'
  We need nor fear, like them, dishonour'd graves.

"All had not fail'd our king, though worldlings base
  Welcome the gloomy Dutchman as their god.
For us, we served through life the Stuart race,
  And neither court nor dread th' Usurper's nod.
We, who disdain'd the stalwart Cromwell's might,
  And braved the scaffold or the dungeon cold—
We, who bear scars from many a glorious fight,
  May not like Churchill spawn be bought with gold.

"Nay, once more for fair France! exile we hail!
  I think the stars look nearer to us there.
The wind blows fresh from shore, let loose the sail!
  Hearts void of guile can find home everywhere.
Poor as of old, when Worcester fight was lost—
  Then a mere stripling, now with grizzled beard—
I share my Sovereign's fate, nor grudge the cost:
  Honour unsmirch'd, nought else in life I fear'd."

Laudator Temporis Acti.

(Cavalier Nonjuror cantat, 1697.)

Closed now the book, displaced the lamp,
   Flung wide the window-shutter;
The night-breeze strikes in cold and damp,
   The fir-trees moan and mutter :
Lo, dawn is near ! pale Student thou
   No count of time hast reckon'd ;
Go, seek a rest for weary brow
   In dreams of Charles the Second.

Sad grows the world : those hours are past
   When jovially convivial
Choice Spirits met, and round them cast
   Such glow as made cares trivial ;
When nights prolong'd through following days
   Found night still closing o'er us,
While Youth and Age exchanged their lays,
   Or intertwin'd in chorus.

Our gravest Pundits of the Bench,
  Right-reverend Sirs of Pulpit,
Smiled at the praise of some coy wench,
  Or—if too warm—could gulp it.
Loyal to King, faithful to Church,
  And firm to Constitution,
Nor friend nor foe they left in lurch,
  Or sneak'd to Revolution.

There many a sage Physician told
  Fresh facts of healing knowledge ;
There, the dazed Bookworm could grow bold,
  And speak of pranks at College :
There, weary Pamphleteers forgot
  Faction, debates, and readers,
But help'd to drain the clinking-pot
  With punning Special-pleaders.

How oft some warrior, famed abroad
  For valour in campaigning,
Exchanged the thrust with foes he awed
  For hob-a-nob Champaigning !
While some old Salt, an admiral
  And circumnavigator,
Join'd in the revel at our call,
  Nor sheer'd-off three days later.

Who lives to thrill with jest and song,
   Like those whose memories haunt us ?—
Who never knew a night too long,
   Or head-ache that could daunt us.
The weaklings of a later day
   Win neither Mirth nor Thinking;
They mix, and spoil, both work and play :
   They have lost the art of drinking I

For me, I lonely grow, and shy,
   No one seems worth my courting,
Though girls have still a laughing eye,
   And tempt to May-day sporting :
For sillier youth, or richer Lord,
   Or some staid prig and colder,
" Neat-handed Phillis" spreads the board,
   And Chloe bares her shoulder.

In days gone by, light grew the task,
   For holidays were glorious,
When brilliant *talk* sublim'd the flask,
   That now is deem'd uproarious.
With so much Puritanic cant,
   Sail-trimmers' bleating drivel,
And yelps of moralizing rant,
   One scarcely can keep civil.

Our politics are insincere,
    For Statesmen cog and shuffle ;
They hit not from the shoulder clear,
    But dodge, and spar with muffle.
How Bench and Bar sink, steep'd in mire,
    Avails not here recording :
While Prelates cannot now look higher
    Than to mere self-rewarding.

Friends of old days, 'tis well you died,
    Before like me you sicken'd
Amid the rottenness and pride
    That in this world have quicken'd :
You pass'd, ere yet your hopes grew dim,
    While Love and Friendship warm'd you :
I look but to th' horizon's rim
    For all that erst had charm'd you.

Not here, amid a lower crew,
    I seek to fill your places ;
For men no more have hearts as true,
    Nor maids—though fair their faces.
My thoughts flit back to earlier days,
    Where Pleasure's finger beckon'd,
Cheer'd with the Beauty, Love, and Lays
    That warm'd our Charles the Second.

Esperanza.

(*Written at Bournemouth, September,* 1884.)

They have pass'd away to the Silent Land,
    The friends of my early days;
When my hair turns grey I shall lonely stand,
    And hear not their words of praise,
With never a son to clasp my hand,
    Or a girl to chant my Lays.

It may be, of all that I tried to do,
    In the life that has ebb'd and gone,
There is little to last till the days grow new,
    Or be told on my burial-stone,
Save the struggle to give a Verdict true
    On the Cavalier Times here shown.

Yet I dare to hope, when my bones are dust,
    That in lands beyond the sea
A race shall arise of a larger trust,
    With a spirit unstained and free,
Who may prize my work as sound and just,
    And cherish my memory.

Cavalier Lyrics.

PART III.—MISCELLANEOUS.

Great cost in sowing, but the harvest small;
Little the shear of wool, with noisiest cry;
Leaves, but no fruit of figs, to taste and try;
* ' Failure and vanity await us all!'*
Wise proverbs, heard so often that they pall,
Yet they dishearten men who once soar'd high,
Ambitious, hopeful, ere their chance slipt by,
* And left them doom'd for life obscure to crawl.*

What wealth of books, what various lands we view'd,
* What friends their hearts gave freely in the Past,*
What harsh experience taught us fortitude,
* What bounties were to us by Nature cast,*
Throughout Youth's seed-time; yet nought hath ensued,
* Save trifling harvest ' Lyrics': these the last.*

L

Mes Amis.

Could I mention all writers I care for,
  Living now, or gone home to their rest,—
Explaining the why and the wherefore
  I cherish of each one his best,
I should need a long list to contain them,
  Not like Lubbock's blind Century roll ;
But my memory still can retain them,
  True physicians of heart, brain, and soul.

Ballade of our Twin Poets.

There are Two who have grown very dear,
   Far above the world's brattle and clang
Their voices sound sweetly and clear,
    Thus we love well each Lyric they sang :
    (Letting Puritan cynics go hang !—
Churls that maunder in prose, sniff or sneer:)
Hail we true friends who came Earth to cheer,
    Austin Dobson and Fife's Andrew Lang !

Art thou old, with thy leaf turning sear?
   Hast thou found thy cup's bitter sharp tang?
Dost thou wait ev'ry night for thy bier,
    As though in the morn death-bells rang?
    Because early in youth some woe stang,
Is thy present hour hopeless and drear?—
Take advice, my good Sage, study here
    Austin Dobson and Fife's Andrew Lang.

Art thou young? Cheeks unwetted by tear,
   Heart unchill'd by the Pessimist gang,
Dost thou welcome each joy of the year?
    Art thou still free from life's *Sturm und Drang*,
    With no deeper remorse or keen pang
Than arises from bacca and beer?—
These two poets prove camerades sincere,
    Austin Dobson and Fife's Andrew Lang.

L'Envoi.

Queen of Beauty, who rulest our sphere,
   To the Laureates of ' Brocade' and ' Hwang'
Grant thy smiles and best words without fear :
    Austin Dobson and Fife's Andrew Lang !

A Leap-Year Birth-Day Ode.

I.

We come to thee, we bring
These flowerets of the Spring,
Pure in their loveliness of maiden bloom ;
And wreathe a coronet,
That on thy brow we set,
A Birth-day gift, to banish care and gloom.

The four-fold years adorn
Thy smiling natal-morn,
In sacred rarity of festival ;
And blend in one alone
The charms of three 'fore-gone,
Twining their memories in a coronal.

Each year of thine doth show
Four Winters white with snow,
Sullen with low'ring skies of coming storm ;
Nor less of Summer's mirth,
In gladness o'er the earth,
To clothe the grove, and living creatures warm.

Four Autumns fade away
From bloom to slow decay,
Their golden banners down the wind they wave ;
And four times must the Spring
In gentle blossoming
Emblem the soul's new birth from wintry grave.

II.

So rich, so mark'd to thee
Each span of life must be,
Though we forget how swift we age and fade ;
Each year whirls round the sun
Our circlet, fully won,
While thine has but a quarter edged from shade.

We read a sweet surprise
In thy soft earnest eyes
Saluting Nature's marvels ever new ;
And watch the dawning bright
That speaks thy soul's delight
In all discern'd by thee of beautiful and true.

Still in thy girlish grace
Childhood's first smile we trace ;
Those who have known thee best, and loved thee long,
Think of thy cradled sleep,
When they calm watch did keep,
Or charm'd thy baby dreams with lulling song :

The small hands crumpled in   1844.
The soft and rosy chin,
The wee ripe lips half-open, warm and red ;
The truant curls that hid
The blue-vein'd closed eyelid,
While on a snow-white pillow lay thy head.

III.

When continental thrones   [1848.
   Toppled o'er cars and stones,
Thy festival raised toys in barricade ;
   Sportively friends were told
   (Although four years had rolled)
Thy claim was but for one true year, fair maid.

   Thy ringing laugh and wile
   Awaken'd answering smile
In all who join'd thy revels, old and young ;
   Of spotless purity
   Sweet omens came to thee,
When emblem snowdrops on thy brow were hung.

   Yet was there shade of change
   Around thee, faces strange,
Mourning the loss of dear ones pass'd to sleep ;
   When thou, in girlish power,   [1852.
   Queen of Bisextile hour,
Thy Second Festival wert called to keep.

   More swiftly roll'd the hours,
   With sunshine and brief showers,
With smiles and tears they brought thy natal-day once more ;
   Pale had'st thou grown, and mild
   With thought, yet still a child,
Musing in silence on life's chequer'd lore.

IV.

Not dazzled or confused,   [1856.
Not spell-bound, scarce amused,
Receiving all impressions silently;
Reading how wondrous are
Dewdrop and leaf and star,
And thine own soul, in solemn majesty.

There had come presages,
And hopeful messages,
Wafted to thee from future hours unborn;
Thrilling thy girlish heart,
Contrasting thy new part,
And future, with the child-life all outworn.

Even now, at "Sweet Sixteen"   [1860.
Of those who still have been
Thy playmates from the cradle to this eve,
We hail thee "aged Four!"
And chant our welcome o'er,
While for thy sake we spring-time garlands weave.

Here at thy feet we lay
Our tribute song this day:
May HE Who sees and loves be ever thy defence!
Bidding thee meekly stand,
A lily in thy hand,
Clothed in the white robes of thy innocence.

(29th of February, 1860.)

My Friend the Actress.

DEAREST FRIEND,—Congratulations, in the usual course of things,
From each casual acquaintance every Post unto thee brings ;
All the round of little visits, when return'd from Wedding Tour,
In acknowledgement of Bride-cake and of cards, await thee sure ;
All the prying observations, all the doubts are satisfied,
Of old histrionic rivals (galled at hailing thee as Bride) :
Since the novelty is ebbing, let me send a tribute line
To the Exile from the Footlights, with a sigh for *auld lang syne*.

Yes, the Exile ! we have lost thee.   Nevermore we thrill to hear
That sweet voice of liquid music at the bedside of King Lear ;
Nevermore the wail of anguish from the bride in Cyprus slain ;
Nevermore Ophelia's madness can draw down our tears again :
Now indeed Fidele 's buried, in the cave where we had seen
All that human grace and beauty could pourtray of Imogine.
Dim the lesser lights that charm'd us, that gave lustre in the gloom,
Cheering daily life around us : nevermore may these relume.
Where is now the ' Laura Leeson,' with her mingled love and pride,
Girlish mirth and woman's sweetness ?   Torn for ever from our side.
Thou hast left us.   In the darken'd hours, that daunt the merriest souls,
Those remembrances are saddest which the pleasant Past unrolls :
When the jaded Theatre-lounger thinks of all he used to see,
Owning ' No one can replace her, to the Drama, or to me !
Not the words and stage-finessing, not the postures glibly taught,
But the soul that shone through action : soul reveal'd in calm of thought ;
That made even old accustom'd censor-cynics young again,
To believe the poet's fancies no chimæra of the brain,
But design'd from living virtues, true affections, such as moved
Her who gave them glow and utterance, from the pages she well loved.'

It is over. The green curtain falls, to hide the faëry scene,
The glass chandelier is lightless, where prismatic gleams had been ;
Now no strain of music lingers, but in dusty corners lie
Kettle-drums and big bass-viols, the dry bones of harmony ;
While some old forgotten playbills, pasted in the gallery stair,
Like the flags in Windsor chapel flutter idly in the air ;
And the scent of mouldy orange-peel and corks of ginger-beer
Hint the mystic words *Sic transit!* better than a sigh or tear :
Thus the name of Harriet Frankland flits for ever from our sphere.

It is idle task, lamenting, but it may our grief assuage
To remember her engagement on a nobler Private Stage :
Though a Star to us, for ever, her *début's* in ' Married Life,'
With the highest range of business in the ' Honeymoon ' and ' Wife.'
If no share in ' Fortune's Frolics ' be her lot, we may be sure
From the ' Comedy of Errors ' she remains for ever pure.
In ' Revenge ' through life deficient, she abandons ' Lovers' Vows,'
Leaves a ' Stranger ' with ' The Critic,' silly ' Rivals,' for ' My Spouse.'
So ' The Wonder ' passes from us ; ' Notoriety's avail
Only serves her future converse as a sort of ' Winter's Tale,'
When ' The Love-Chase ' and its ' Tempest ' may her mirthful hours
    regale.

But to me? Ah, dew-eyed Memory, wherefore dwell on lovelier hours
With one thought of self to canker all that garland twine of flowers ?
Can'st thou hear the full voice rolling, with its echoes from the lore
Of her cherish'd Bards, and mourn lest thou may'st hear it nevermore ?
See ! again in wonted circlets play her fingers on the chords,
And her blue eyes wake to rapture, at the spell of poets' words ;
And the deep true heart of Woman beats within the loveliest breast
That had ever heav'd to sorrow, or affection e'er impress'd.
Let who will enclasp that treasure, from my heart no pang can tear
The remembrances and friendship that must always keep her dear :
May God bless her ! and His Angels ever minist'ring be near.

In the West.

Light fall the dews upon thy grave,
  Though tears no more are shed for thee !
Sternly the Future now we brave,
  Dearer thou art to memory.
But we have learnt to mask the grief
  That sapp'd our strength—that crush'd our joy,
Or in a holier rapt belief
  Seek peace, where Death cannot destroy.

All things have changed since thou did'st fade,
  No love so true might bloom again ;
None by our side for long had stayed,
  Gentle yet firm, in doubt and pain ;
None loving, faithful, like to thee,
  Unselfish in thy sweet pure trust,
Smiling and meek in misery :
  O God ! to think thou art but dust.

We know that under this green turf
  Lies all we once could touch and see ;
While we are rotting in the surf—
  The slime of earth, thou art set free :
Free from the chains that curb us still,
  Binding the soul to ways impure ;
The stubborn pride no stroke can kill,
  The weak defence when sins allure.

Shall not this bondage break at last ?
  These bitter memories quit the breast ?
No backward glance should now be cast,
  Save when it seeks thy place of rest.
Now let the onward path be trod
  Not for our own vile gain or bliss,
But for the glory of that God
  Who took thee to His world, from this.

On the Coast of Cornwall.

(At the Land's End, September, '73.)

Poets may sing of their Haunted Spring,
  With fairy or wood-nymph near ;
Hunters may tell of flood and fell,
  In their far North, chasing the deer ;
Bucks growing old may dislike water cold,
  If not ' laced ' with *eau de vie :*
The Bishop cries "Zounds ! a Priest follow hounds !"
  But for me there's no joy like the Sea.

Dull cynics may sneer at the Marinere
  Who lives on the briny wave ;
He as happy is found, as in toil underground
  Lives our Cornish tin-miner brave.
Life is pleasant enough, when the waves are rough,
  And the winds are whistling free,
If we swing on these rocks, amid billowy shocks,
  And feel a new life by the Sea.

No hermit am I, my race to decry,
  And sulk in a solitude ;
I like theatres, *on dits*, and big libraries
  (With all Cavalier tastes imbued) :
I prize the wiles of maiden-smiles,
  And the prattle of Infancy :
But of all, the best I count a rest
  By the side of our friend the Sea.

Dame Nature well knew what suited you
  And me, fellow-Englishman !
Whom she caused to be born, some far-back morn,
  Where Neptune the coast might span.
Whatever our toil, we slip off the coil,
  And regain lost jollity,
When we seek the strand of our native land,
  Finding Rest beside the Sea.

Richard of Rochester.

(*The English Savonarola, Pre-Deformation time*, circa 1407.)

[*Rotuli Collegii Nirgensiensi*, xviii. *cap.* 8. *Nota* c.]

If I could sing, or touch the string,
   Make quavers and big crotchets stir,
I'd strive to tell, with organ swell,
   Of Richard, monk at Rochester :
Unyielding, brave, of manner grave,
   Though somewhat Theophrastical,
He rais'd a stir and sharp demur
   'Mong folks ecclesiastical.

His " Life and Times " our ballad-rhymes
   Inadequately celebrate :
He lonely stood in doing good,
   (Like most brave men, strict celibate :)
He had no spouse, but kept his vows
   Immaculate, with ne'er a ' niece '
(Priests had such then), whom other men
   Called daughter—Maud or Bérenice.

He preach'd, we're told, in language bold,
   Dealt right and left some ' staggerers,'
Religion's foes he doom'd to woes,
   Oppressors, curs, and swaggerers :
Like one inspired he spoke, thus fired
   By truth, not jerks professional ;
And ne'er betray'd of man or maid
   The secrets of Confessional.

By words well-timed, he might have climb'd
   To high seats apostolical ;
Or crack'd his jest, among the rest,
   To whom Life was a frolic all :
But he disdain'd low arts, and gain'd
   A higher throne than Prelates give ;
His prayers all meant, " May we repent ! "
   While others hiccough'd, " Boys, let's live ! "

He trod the floor with rich or poor,
   Clasp'd hands with serf or Lady fair ;
As one who knew their value true,
   Above false shows of May-day glare ;
And when grim Death would stop their breath,
   In lowliest cot or battle-field,
He sought the shriven to fit for heaven :
   While smug divines vain prattle yield.

No pamperer, he, of luxury,
   In self or neighbours : " Body down ! "
His exhortation through the nation,
   " Conquer thy-Self ! No cross, no crown ! "
Clearly he spoke, and echoes woke
   In living hearts, the best applause ;
Thus helped to raise, for better days,
   A race to honour Love and Laws.

Search till you're blind, you will not find
   His tomb at Rochester adorn'd :
'Neath Molash yews, kept moist by dews
   And loving tears, men laid him, mourn'd.   [Ch. p. 16.]
His writings few, but each word true,
   Printed on soul and memory,
Not mouldy book. Far may we look
   Ere we find Churchmen brave as he.

Grandfather.

(Felis Catus domestica, obiit Julij, 1862, *ætatis* 22.)

'Life to the last enjoy'd' here Pussy lies,
Renown'd for mousing, and for catching flies ;
Loving o'er grass and pliant branch to roam,
Yet ever constant to the smiles of home ;
Philosopher of Garden and of Porch,
Whom sun and hearth had warm'd, but could not scorch.
Monarchs might envy him his regal fur,
And list the music of his household purr.
For sweet content possess'd his feline soul,
When milk of human kindness brim'd the bowl :
Nor anger nor ingratitude e'er shed
The blood of hand that strok'd him or that fed.
Blameless in morals, fear'd by mice and rats,
The *Preux Chevalier* of the race of cats,
He has outliv'd their customary span,
As Jenkins and Old Parr had that of man.
He might on tiles have murmur'd, in moonshine,
Nestorian tales of youth and Troy divine ;
Of rivals fought ; of kitten-martyrdoms ;
While meekly listening round sat Tabs and Toms :
But, with the modesty of genuine worth,
He vaunted not his deeds of ancient birth,
His whiskers twitch'd not at the world's applause,
He only yawn'd, and lick'd his reverend paws,
Curl'd round his head his tail, then fell asleep,
Lapp'd in sweet dreams, and left us here to weep :
    Yet know we well that, ere he sank to rest,
    So far as mortal cats are, 'Grandfather' was blest.

Trap.

(Died at Margate, January 10, 1880, aged 16 years.)

Buried at Updown, Isle of Thanet.

Faithful and kind ! we need not bring,
To deck thee, flowerets of the Spring ;
Enwreath'd already by the snow
Is the calm spot where thou liest low :
The birds that twitter on each stem
Around thee sing thy Requiem,
And every loving heart shall keep
Thy memory green, while thou dost sleep.
  No harsher doom may us behap,
   Than thus to meet grim Death, like ' Trap.'

Le Printemps fait l'Esperance.

L'Eté pour moi fait la Joie.

A Year's Messages.

(1883.)

I.—THE CHIME OF BELLS.

No sportive peal of wedding-bells
  To hail the New Year's birth we give :
Sadly funereal tolling dwells
  In memory still with us who live.

Rest and be thankful, while you may ;
  Rise and be active, if you can ;
Sing and rejoice, or mourn and pray ;
  But helm'd and arm'd, be still a man.

No coward, crouching 'neath the thong ;
  No tyrant o'er thy fellow-slave ;
But a brave warrior against wrong,
  With equal scorn for fool or knave.

So shall thy year be ever new,
  And Time bear record thou hast trod
The chosen pathway, firm and true,
  That leads man onward, nearer God.

II.—FEBRUARY. (SPRING-FLOWERS.)

Again they bloom, the flowers we love,
　They pierce the mould, they laugh at snow,
And in each hedgerow, dell or grove,
　Smile in our face where'er we go.

Fragile as childhood, but as strong
　To conquer where brute force were vain,
Be these our theme of joyful song :
　The flowers that brighten earth again.

They wreathe the brow, they deck the breast,
　They make the poorest home grow gay ;
Thank God for these among the rest,
　The flowers that cheer us on our way.

III.—MARCH WINDS.

How shall we welcome thee, thou wind,
   Blowing across the moor we love?
Sportive betimes, fierce or unkind,
   We fear thee not, where'er we rove.

Tame languor lulls to slothful ease,
   Cowards and slaves from idlesse grow;
We better love the friendly breeze
   That smites our cheek to healthy glow.

Ours is no land for Sybarites,
   To sink supine when harsh winds drive;
But Freedom in our storms delights,
   Knowing they teach us how to strive.

Then welcome be the angry gales!—
   Welcome as are the Zephyrs rare
That scantly fill our summer sails
   When rippling waves are bright and fair.

IV.—April. (Childhood.)

Like Childhood, with its giddy mirth,
  Sweet April always seems to be ;
With tear-drops, sunny from their birth,
  Ready to fall 'mid heartiest glee.

Little reveal'd of solemn cares
  Promise and threat together blent ;
Lightest of burdens yet she bears,
  Counting it sport, she smiles content.

Happy the dawn of life should be,
  Ere toil begins to weigh us down ;
Then prize the joys of Infancy,
  Nor sternly at the follies frown.

Wiser that unregardful child
  Than Age with all its doubt and care ;
Such love, unbought and unbeguil'd,
  Brings sweeter gifts for earth to wear.

V.—MAY. (SONG-BIRDS.)

Birds that I love, and feed, but never slew,
    That twitter round me fearless, knowing well
I harm you not; that brush the morning dew,
    And hymn your gladness where I chance to dwell;
Long may your blithe endearments give me peace,
    Freely careering round me, welcom'd friends;
Loved must you be, till life's brief summer cease;
    Yea, till its drearier winter also ends.
Who grudge you 'crumbs of comfort,' fruit purloin'd,
    Or seeds unearth'd in busy quest, are churls!
They cannot weigh a treasure save when coin'd:
    Your songs, your flights, your plumes are unpriz'd pearls.
Shame on your ruthless murderers! who wear
    Th' accusing feathers pluck'd from out your wings,
To deck their own false curls of purchas'd hair:
    Accurs'd, though conscience neither speaks nor stings.

VI.—JUNE.   (J. S. B.)

Almost I fear, O Love ! to speak my cares :
   Thou slumberest so lightly that my breath
Is hush'd in tenderness, and whisper'd prayers
   Befit thy couch, or silence mute as death.
Sleep, is it still, that binds thee?   Long I've seen
   Thine eyelids closed, missing the light that shone,
So prized of yore.   Ah me ! how can I wean
   My thoughts from dread that thou art from me gone ?
Is it too late to woo thee back to life ?
   Thou can'st not know how weary and how sad
This hopeless vigil grows : while hateful strife
   Tempts like relief from anguish, motley-clad.
Wake, Love, if pulse still beat, if breath inspire,
   And thou art not mere shadow of a Dream !—
Could I have linger'd by th' extinguish'd fire,
   That once had warm'd, without one faintest gleam ?

VII.—JULY. (VIBRATIONS.)

You have haunted my life, O Music sweet !
  Till now when I'm turning grey ;
I never fear'd sorrow or wrath to meet
  While you could my ills allay.
Though treachery stabb'd behind my back,
  And friendship grew timid or cold,
While I scorn'd Ambition's tangled track,
  Or the miser's greed for gold ;
Though prudence turn'd pale at shadowy risk,
  When the whisper of sloth grew bold ;
And hatred gleam'd vengeful, a basilisk,
  Till we loath'd the life half-told :
No foes could conquer the living faith,
  Or one charm of the echoing lyre :
I laugh to scorn what the false world saith,
  While Music still bids aspire.

VIII.—AUGUST. (VOX STELLARUM.)

Ye were nearer of old, ye Stars of night,
　　Ye were near us, when young and free
We floated away on your beams of light
　　In the dreams of infancy.

We fear'd no millions of miles between,
　　For little of Science we knew ;
But, loving to watch your silvery sheen,
　　We long'd to soar to you.

Then as years roll'd by, in foreign lands
　　Where all things else were changed,
Ye were still the same, over desert sands,
　　Or the mountains where we ranged.

Now, whether we dwell on the moor or fen,
　　Or imprison'd in squalid town,
It is little we heed th' encircling men,
　　While you on our sleep look down.

IX.—September. (Twilight.)

Almost gone by, our Summer-time of flowers,
  The brightness, warmth, and gladness of the sky ;
The song of birds, thrilling the pleasant hours,
  With hymns of joy : ah ! swiftly flitting by.

Almost gone by, the dreamy lingering twilight,
  Drowsing the earth with blessing from on high ;
Sportive May-morn, noon lustrous in July-light,
  Or regal August-eve : too soon gone by !

Gone by, gone by, Love's freshness, hope, and laughter ;
  Long ere the Summer close, our raptures fly :
Stern courage, patience, faith in times hereafter,
  These, God be thank'd ! are with us till we die.

X.—October. (Friends.)

Fool ! who would scorn as lonely this our cell—
　As dim, the student's lamp-light that illumes
So vast a concourse of the ghosts who dwell
　In Fields Elysian, not in rifled tombs :

All the dead Sages live for us, our friends ;
　They call us to them, and themselves oft come
To give their counsel : Beauty too attends :
　And Heroes, from their sacred martyrdoms.

We count it wiser choice to love the lore
　Of ancient days, than join the restless crowd,
Who deem their present life all lives before,
　And in their ignorance are glibly proud.

Spread to our eyes are banquets of past time ;
　Was it great loss, abstaining from new feast ?
We hear the echoes of Old Poets' rhyme :
　Miss we the babble of your new high priest ?

XI.—November. (Memories.)

If we grow weary, ere our day is spent,
  And action prove more idle than our dream ;
If progress has but led to discontent,
  And all that *is*, or shall be, cheerless seem,—

How can we draw from memories of the Past
  Fresh energy to help us now fight on ?
While old experience, with its treasures vast,
  Shows many a hope's defeat, few victories won ?

Let others boast they wiser grow with years,
  And scornfully decry their youthful aims ;
For me, remembrance brings them back with tears,
  And silenced voices yield beloved acclaims.

Let the new wrestlers strive for each new crown :
  These gain the triumph, those the pang who lose.
Life wanes : we heed applause no more than frowns,
  No myrtle-bowers yield peace like churchyard yews !

XII.—DECEMBER.　(THE UNSEEN END.)

Why linger, then, since Life is on the lees?
　　Youth's golden Treasure-store is spent and gone;
Few are the leaves left trembling on the trees;
　　Carve the last verses thus on the head-stone :—

Say, " It was rich in blessings, our old life;
　　From a full chalice once the draught was quaff'd;
Pure was the love for maiden, child, and wife;
　　Friends, fellow-pilgrims, with us mourn'd or laugh'd.

" Never the dullness of the crowd could blight
　　The soul that found refreshment everywhere,
From History's scroll, from Science' clearer light,
　　From birds, from music, and from all things fair.

" Enough of wood-walks, flower-begirt, for those
　　Who felt their step turn feeble, eyes grow dim;
Let the Unseen be welcome at the close,
　　Since all here seen had drawn us nearer HIM."

L'Automne donne l'abondance.

L'Hiver apprends de se reconnaître.

Lady Fairfax.

(*Anne Vere, wife of Sir Thomas Fairfax, Obiit* 16 *Oct.*, 1665.)

" A Vere—a Fairfax—honour's honour she."

Though she was not accounted a Cavalier Dame,
   Or a Beauty to catch the eye,
We hold in our heart her stainless name,
   And praise her for courage high,
Since she boldly avow'd her sense of shame
   When they doom'd King Charles to die ;
She rejoiced that her ' Black Tom ' shared no blame :
   " He's well quit of such company ! "
Proudly felt he, when he homeward came,
   And learnt what his wife dared cry.

Lady Bountiful.

What time the world, to merit dull,
   Applauded wolves that ravage herds,
Her heart of generous warmth was full,
   But wasted not her love in words :
She would have night-cap'd Yorick's skull,
   And knitted socks for Humming-birds.

Under the Molash Yews.

Under the Molash Yews,
When Spring flowers come again, are children sporting,
While youthful lovers linger, coyly courting ;
So sweetly dream they of their future days,
So brightly sunshine on the green turf plays,
> None can a smile refuse,
> Under our Molash Yews.

Under the Molash Yews,
Summer brings back again, for rest and pleasure,
Our parted wayfarers, in scanty leisure ;
Leaning on rustic stile, sighing, they wonder
What worthless spell had held them long asunder.
> No worldly cares confuse
> Under our Molash Yews.

Under the Molash Yews,
When Autumn fills the harvest-fields with labour,—
When Hop-grounds ring with mirth, till pipe and tabor
Sound in the early twilight through green lanes,
Where mothers homeward haste, counting their gains :
> Soft fall the chilly dews,
> Under our Molash Yews.

Under the Molash Yews,
When Winter snow has hush'd the busy village,
And bound the fields from every tread and tillage,
One darken'd grave 'mid the white mounds doth wait
The wearied Pilgrim, borne to the Lych-gate :
> Earth claims her wonted dues,
> Under the Molash Yews.

Epitaphium Tibi Auctoris.

(Sine die notavit.)

Underneath this sod or stone,
Wave or sand (to him all's one,
Since his little life is done),
Joseph Woodfall Ebsworth lies,
Whom, if you so please, you prize,
Ere his time to wake and rise.

Life he well enjoyed, good sooth !
Kept in age the heart of youth,
Loving One with changeless truth :
(In his breast was room for more,
Let us say, at least a score,)
With big tomes of ballad-lore.

Others grasp at power or wealth,
He chose study, calm, and health,
Slipt through life as though by stealth :
Thus, mayhap ! was known to few,
For he was not oft on view—
Never once was seen by you ?

Bards and Critics nowadays
Haunt too much the public ways,
Where a crowd of gossips gaze.
He made choice to lonely tread
Shy field-pathways, flower bespread ;
Half forgotten, 'live or dead.
 Need no more of him be said.

Finis.

Who will, may foot it here with me :
  Come, sound the pipe and tabor !
Welcome awaits and jollity,
  For stranger as for neighbour.
Fling politics aside, brave boys !
  Leave dross of wealth, more trivial :
Take your true holiday in joys
  Unselfish and convivial.

We raise our Maypole in the Strand,
  Amid the crowd and coaches ;
No Hermit's choice, but hand in hand
  With each nymph who approaches ;
Whether a Lely-painted Dame,
  Adorn'd from crest to shoe-tie,
Or a blithe Milkmaid : all the same,
  If bright with youth and beauty.

We sang of battles, plots and schemes;
    Trod at Court-Balls grave measure;
We call'd you back to Poets' dreams,
    Basking in sunny leisure.
Our First Part mark'd rebellious strife
    Of Cromwell; but ' Old Rowley'
Our Second claim'd, for maid and wife,
    Buxom, or pert, or holy.

Frolic and Fun our lives prolong,
    Well for us if we prize them;
No less we strive 'gainst sloth or wrong;
    And as for foes—despise them.
Join these our gambols, Cavaliers,
    And Primrose Dames, benignants!
Honour the courage of past years,
    When we were styled ' Malignants.'

NOTES.

Preface, p. xxi.—It is time to renew the preliminary announcement, made in 1881, of our projected work (delayed by successive issues of *Bagford* and *Roxburghe Ballads*, nearly completed, for the Ballad Society).

In our coming book, giving (unmutilatedly) *The Ballads, Songs, and Political Poems of the Civil Wars, the Commonwealth, and the Restoration*, from 1637 to 1661 (now far advanced in MSS., and soon to seek acceptance of a wider public, in England and America), an important period of our past national existence will be illustrated in detail. We hope to show the daily life and difficulties of citizen and soldier, of churchman and of sectary, of loyal Cavalier and of factious Regicide. The strife still maintained between opposed camps, the stifling heat of controversy from fires kindled by irreconcileable antagonisms, may be better understood, whether good or evil, after the similar excitement of an earlier time has been traced, with the consequences of defective reasoning, blind prejudice, insane hatred, and intolerance.

So long as our country maintains vigour the Great Rebellion must hold a chief place in our study. Of late, it is true, little wisdom has been shown in the partizanship and malevolence with which the events of that time have been misrepresented, to suit the views of political revolutionists or their reactionary foes. Leaders and followers in the earlier struggle have had their worst faults excused

or their best virtues decried, their characters alternately
white-washed by sycophants or blackened by slanderers,
in obedience to party spite and ambition. Not truth has
been sought, but sectarian victories. Degenerating from
patriotism to selfishness, statesmen often forget the
Empire in pursuit of place. The old party-cries yet
lingering excite the accustomed passion, until progress
itself becomes doubtful. Church and State alike defied,
by utter lawlessness; privilege or prerogative, aggressive
nonconformity and uncompromising loyalty; parliamentary
incompetence, with many spasms of tyranny, unable to
compass its end; civic greed united with parsimony; blunt
country honesty and insincere courtly elegance, will in
turn be presented for consideration in each contemporary
mirror of bygone times; the street ballad broadside, the
secretly whispered lampoon, and the gay lyrics that were
sung by brave fighters or fair damsels in the England
of two hundred years ago.

The title will probably be, simply THE CIVIL WARS
AND THE PROTECTORATE, UNTIL THE RESTORATION;
ILLUSTRATED BY THE BALLADS AND POEMS OF THE
TIME. To this (as recorded so early as nine years ago,
November, 1877,) J. W. Ebsworth devotes the remaining
years of his life; if any years remain to be given.

    ⁎⁎ Each Division will be self-complete, issued in chronological
order, probably in halves or half-annually. Thus the first portion
(virtually ready in manuscript) is devoted to the time between the
outbreak of the Scotch Rebellion, 'the Bishops' War,' and the judicial
murder of Archbishop Laud; an important period in Ecclesiastical
history.

    The Second Part continues the military history, from the raising of
the Standard at Nottingham, until the trial and death of Charles I.

The Third Part extends to the dissolution of the Long Parliament, April 20, 1653.

The Fourth Part, with the Protector as its central figure, should end with the great storm of September, 1658, in which the soul of Oliver Cromwell passed away.

The Fifth and last Division should give the events of the two years following his death, including the expiring struggles of 'the Rump' and the anarchists, the Restoration, and the execution of the Regicides.

The whole series to be illustrated with copies of the contemporary caricatures and portraits. Obtainable only from the Editor.

Preface, p. xxv.—The mention of Mr. William Morris Wood, of Hertford, gives occasion to add a few words of eulogy to the class of 'Readers for the Press,' whereof he is a most worthy ornament. How much all authors owe to him and his brethren, patient and assiduous and skilful, is seldom remembered. In his honour we wrote,

Der Einige.

Though long I claim'd for Cavaliers
   'Gainst scandal to be pleader,
I am content if all these years
   I found one 'Constant Reader.'

None else so good as mine men boast,
   (Be hush'd, ye scornful hinters !)
My constant reader's worth your host :
   But *he* reads——for the Printers.

If ordinary readers wish to see the Odes of Typographical Laudation, rendered by us to the Hertford compositors, reader, and pressmen of Messrs. Stephen Austin and Sons, at successive *wayzgoose* feasts, some may be found inserted among our *Roxburghe Ballads*.

Page 10 —*Epitaph on John Mottesfont.* The translation in rhymed verse, by "E. J. B., Lydd, 1845," is here reprinted (from *The Kentish Garland* of Miss De Vaynes, p. 750, printed by Messrs. Austin, 1882) :

"Do thou, the tombs beholding here, count the world's pleasure nought :
To such a dwelling place as mine shall ev'ry man be brought.
The majesty of mighty kings, all worldly pomp and power,
Shall pass away without delay in death's destructive hour.

Behold a crown to none is given, unless with care he tread
The just man's path, and sinner's ways avoid with fear and dread.
O who may tell how great their wealth who heavenly kingdoms gain,
Their bliss reveal who know and feel all earthly things are vain?"

Cavaliers would reverently, or irreverently (*suum cuique*), respond
with their jovial *refrain* of " *Which nobody can deny !*" The translation
(and our own answer, following p. 331), first appeared in *Notes and
Queries*, 6th Series, vol. ii. p. 166 ; during the Editorship of Mr. Turle,
who succeeded Dr. Doran, and preceded the genial Joseph Knight,
present editor (1886).

Future antiquaries cannot fail to turn delightedly to this curious
repository of enquiries, answers, and competitive annotation, whether
of history, literature, gossipry and bibliography, or what our friend, the
late W. J. Thoms, F.S.A. (its first editor), happily called 'Folk-lore.'

The Treasure House for After-time.

Happy are those who write no line,
    But buy each five years ' Series,'
And keep from premature decline
    Our old friend's *Notes and Queries*.

For them no vacant hour is dull,
    They've matters for reflection,
Pages of wit and wisdom full :
    Unequalled choice collection !

P. 13.—*Sir John Suckling's Troop of Horse*. They were (like the
classical birds, baked in a pie) "a dainty dish to set before the king,"
and cost the loyal Sir John 36,000*l*. to caparison and keep them. But
'caparisons are odious,' as Mrs. Malaprop did *not* say. After all the
ridicule encountered by those spruce coxcombs, known as 'the Suckle-
tonian faction,' it is well to remember that their misbehaviour was in

companionship with the then-existing English army, sent against the Scots. Arundel, the commander, deserves the blame. There was no heart in the expedition. Later the civil-war became a stern embittered contest of dauntless courage, but lax discipline, on the part of the Cavaliers. Too late, the brutalities and treacheries of the Cromwellian leaders roused our loyal men for vengeance. If there had remained a Strafford to lead them, defeat would have been impossible. Nothing can extenuate the conduct of Charles I. in signing Sir Thomas Wentworth's death-warrant, after having lured him into danger by the most solemn protestations. Weakness caused vacillation and treachery. The King's own after-fate was a befitting retribution: the Eumenides tracked him, as surely as they followed the assassins of Ibycus :—

> " But woe to him for whom we weave
>   The doom for deeds that shun the light ;
> Fast to the murderer's feet we cleave,
>   The fearful Daughters of the Night."

> Doch wehe, wehe, wer verstehlen
>   Des Mordes schwere That vollbracht ;
> Wir heften uns an seine Sohlen,
>   Das furchtbare Geschlecht der Nacht !

We may be sure that Charles remembered Strafford's solitary reproach, " Put not your trust in Princes !" when he himself read the words in his prayer-book on *the thirtieth morning of the month*, Psalm cxlvi., in that final January. Kismet.

P. 17.—*Maid Marion* is no lineal descendant of the lady closely connected with Robin Hood (whether lawfully Countess of Huntingdon or not deponent is unable to swear confidently), but possibly an ancestress of the " Little Star of Boston," mentioned in the Chronicles of Nirgends College, and *Karl's Legacy*, Tom. ii. pp. 162 to 166.

P. 32.—*Sir Thomas Browne.* It may be better to give our tribute to this noble thinker and worthy man in the form we have adopted, than attempt laboriously to defend his memory against the ungenerous rhetorical assaults of one whom we in general respect and love, the late Lord Lytton (whose translation from Schiller we employ above, and) who declared that the author of *Religio Medici* "had no sympathy with the great business of men" (*Edinburgh Review*, October, 1836). Let it suffice to remember that in his active life as a physician, added to his solitary intellectual studies, there was enough of urgent daily work to be done; without any necessity for abandoning such useful labour in order to join the crowd of declaimers and rufflers, who were engaged in civil-war. He anticipated Goethe's practical wisdom : 'Do the nearest work with energy.'

P. 35.—'*Black Tom*,' the well-known sobriquet of Sir Thomas Fairfax, on whose reputation the only indelible stain is the having yielded to the bitter malignancy of Ireton, by conniving at the cold-blooded murder of Sir Charles Lucas and Sir George Lisle after the surrender of Colchester. Lady Fairfax's spirited exclamations before the falsely-constituted 'High Court of Justice,' that made a pretence of legal trial when packed to condemn Charles I. to death, must ever preserve her memory. She is not named in the earlier pages of the lyrics, owing to the lines (on p. 174) not having been written in time for insertion according to date. She was daughter of Lord Vere, of Tilbury, and married on June 20, 1637. Clements R. Markham tries to insinuate doubts of Clarendon's account being true, but he is himself of no weight and authority, being retained by the other faction.

Gladly would we celebrate such heroines as Charlotte de Tremouille, the heroic defender of Lathom House, or that tender and fragile lily, the Princess Elizabeth, who bent and broke under iniquitous imprisonment at Carisbrook (died Sept. 8, 1650), to whose memory our beloved Queen raised a monument of touching beauty, representing the girl as when found dead, with her head resting on her Bible. The Cavalier ladies deserve a volume to themselves.

P. 50.—'*Dormer's Green*' coincides with the village now called Bessel's Green, in the immediate neighbourhood of the memorable Ide Hill, of which for seventeen years the vicarage was held by the late Rev. A. J. Woodhouse, M.A., near Sundridge and Sevenoaks, Kent. The lines were written August 14, 1868.

P. 51.—Tea-drinking and coffee-drinking were beginning to win favour in London at this date, 1656. Tea is said to have been sold at from 6*l.* to 10*l.* a pound. Samuel Pepys records his first cup of tea on 25 September, 1660, "I did send for a cup of tee (a China drink) of which I never had drank before, and went away" (*Diary*, i. 192, Mynors Bright's edition, 1875). "*The Mercurius Politicus*" of September 30th, 1658, sets forth : "That excellent, and by all physicians approved, China drink, called by the Chineans Tcha, by other nations Tay alias Tee, is sold at the Sultaness Head Coffee House in Sweetings Rents, by the Royal Exchange, London." "Coffee, chocolate, and a kind of drink called *tee*, sold in almost every street in 1659.—Rugge's *Diurnal*." (*Haydn's Dates*, p. 504, 14th ed.)

Coffee seems, earlier than tea, to have become a cheap and accepted beverage, the first coffee-house in London being opened in George Street, Lombard Street, in 1652, and the Rainbow coffee-house, Temple Bar, was represented as a nuisance in 1657. (*Ibid.*, p. 165.)

P. 60.—We entertain no doubt concerning Cromwell's state of mind, his grief and half-stifled remorse after the death of his favourite daughter Elizabeth, Mrs. Claypole, at Hampton Court, on 6th August, 1658, at the age of twenty-nine. We need not here repeat what we already tried to say in the Introduction to *Choyce Drollery*, 1876 (pp. xxii to xxv), in recognition of Elizabeth Claypole's excellence, and of the virtues or vices of Oliver Cromwell. Alongside of him we see how base in comparison were most of his associates.

Page 95.—*The Pantiles* is the name given to the ('paved gutter') walk in front of the Bath-room, Tunbridge Wells, as shown in Walker's engraving. Chloe recalls the Phillis of "They tell me I proved unkind to my lass." Phillis came a century later, but found a celebrator earlier than our Chloe.

P. 96.—John Evelyn records (*Diary and Correspondence*, iv. 26, ed. 1879) the loss of valuable manuscripts, autograph letters from Mary Queen of Scots written to Elizabeth and to Leicester during her imprisonment, etc., which he had weakly lent to Burnet, and could never recover, "are pretended to have been lost at the presse." Wherever we track this Scotch libeller, whom William rewarded with the English bishopric of Salisbury, his utter worthlessness reveals itself.

P. 106.—'*Madam Carwell*' was the common appellation whereby Louise de Quérouaille, the Duchess of Portsmouth, was known, her foreign name being found difficult to pronounce. Her fickleness and prodigality, with the splendour of her Whitehall lodgings, were proverbial.

P. 104.—The author gives his copy of a contemporary copper-plate showing the brutal murder of Archbishop Sharp, by the confederated Covenanters, John Balfour of Burghley, Hackston of Rathillet, etc. The popular belief found utterance in verses on the same broadside, which have been already reprinted in *The Roxburghe Ballads*, iv. 150, 1881, edited by the present writer. The portrait sketch of James Sharp, and also a reduced sketch of the bas-relief on James Sharp's monument, at St. Andrews, are added on p. 105. In passing we protest against the malevolent comments of Osmund Airy, in his Lauderdale Papers of our Camden Society. He is beside himself with spite against Sharp, and carries more sail than cargo. He actually believes in the truthfulness of Gilbert Burnet!

P. 109.— *The Roxburghe Ballads*. We may be forgiven for drawing attention to our own labours in illustrating the court intrigues as well as the street literature of Charles the Second's reign, in volumes IV., V., and VI. of the Roxburghe Ballads, printed for a very limited number of subscribers by the Ballad Society, and still in progress, but near completion. The Treasurer and Hon. Secretary is Mr. William A. Dalziel, of 67, Victoria Road, Finsbury Park, London, N., and the subscription one guinea per annum. (This is mentioned for the Society's sake; the Editors working gratuitously.)

P. 116.—*Alsatia, after Nightfall.* The privileges of sanctuary enjoyed and misused at Whitefriars, commonly called Alsatia (as being a border-land where the rights of property were no more respected than they had been in the original Alsace of Louis XIV.—or since), were abolished by William III., in 1697. He discountenanced all lawlessness except his own, and the acts of his swaggering Dutch hirelings. The flash lingo current, or thieves' Latin, differed not widely from the pattern made early familiar in John Awdeley's *Caveat or Warening for Common Cursetors*, 1567, and his *Fraternitye of Vagabonds*, 1561-1575; argot partly reappearing in *Bacchus and Venus*, 1737, and elsewhere. A few of the words and phrases were subjoined to the printed quartos of "The Squire of Alsatia," Thomas Shadwell's lively comedy, in 1688. We have for several years intended to bring out a carefully edited reprint of all Tom Shadwell's dramatic works, by private subscription. Also *John Cleaveland's Works*, and *Samuel Butler's*. But life slips fast away, "and lo! the little touch, and youth is gone!"

'Rigging' means raiment or apparel?—'garnish' is money paid on entry, fee of 'footing' or propitiatory tribute, as in prison life of old ; 'Black Will' was the serviceable ruffian mentioned by John Wilmot, Earl of Rochester, as being ready to respond with his cudgel to John Dryden's (supposed) satire, in the Rose-Alley outrage of 18 December, 1679. The Mint held similar privileges with those of Whitefriars. 'Tat-mongers' were gambling cheats using false dice, Riot followed any entry of constables into the sacred regions of ruffianism. 'Putts' and 'cullies' meant gulls or victims of cheats. The 'Fifth Monarchy-men,' who tried to renew rebellion soon after the Restoration (and thus in great part justified the harshness of legal punishment dealt out to the regicides), had not died out, but began to emerge boldly from their lurking holes at the time of the Rye House Plot in 1683. 'Knights of the Post' were the perjurers and sham-witnesses, who leaned against posts, ready to be hired, near the courts of justice. 'Stags' were tip-staves or sheriff's-officers. 'Morts' from 'Lightskirts' scarcely differ in kind, only in disputation. 'Apple-squires' were the bullies held in pay at houses of disreputable character. A glimpse of such neighbours is shown in our *Amanda Group of Bagford Poems* and *Drolleries*.

Pages 121 and 129.—Ballads illustrating the Frost Fair on the Thames, in February, 1684 (and also those earlier issued throughout the excitement of the Sham Popish Plot of 1678, and the Rye House Plot of 1683), are given *in extenso* in our Roxburghe Ballads, already mentioned. Though commonly cited by that name, because of having been in the collection of John, the fourth Duke of Roxburghe (except the supplementary Vol. IV., which was gathered by Benjamin Heywood Bright, after he had purchased the other three at the great Roxburghe sale in 1812), the collection had previously, from April, 1773, belonged to Major Thomas Pearson, who died in 1788 (bears his monogram on the title-pages) ; still earlier to James West, Pres. Royal Society ; and originally to Robert Harley, Earl of Oxford, whose name it ought to bear, if justice were done. The ballads had been purchased for him by the celebrated or notorious John Bagford (*b.* 1650—*d.* 1716), who conveyed title-pages and frontispieces, wherever he could find them, as a Hieland reiver would have 'lifted' cattle. Bagford was a professional trafficker in books and prints, often journeying abroad in pursuit of bargains. He made a special collection in three volumes of broadside ballads, which still bear his name at the British Museum. He was a cheery good-natured fellow, somewhat illiterate, and absolutely unscrupulous, but indefatigable in pursuit of his favourite game, for which he beat covers and competitors. (Compare pp. 194, 195.)

P. 134.—The meeting from which John Evelyn had returned was one of the Royal Society (founded 1662), whereof Samuel Pepys had twice been President (1684-85). Charles the Second had always taken a warm interest in science and from the first gave his sanction. Sir Isaac Newton gave his MS. of the *Principia* to the Royal Society in April, '87.

P. 124.—*Trifling with Love* may perhaps irritate persons who know nothing of the Trowbesh Manuscripts, and their wrath may not detect

An Open Secret.

If the Reader (*sans* Anagram) wishes to stop,
Let him ponder these words, "Awld fool, rob the Jew's shop!"

P. 140.—*Laudator Temporis Acti*. If anybody is so foolish as to imagine that the author favours melancholic maunderings, because of things having gone wrong in Stuart days, with defeats in battles, confiscations, impoverishments and butcheries, thus worrying people outrageously who might as well have been happy—such a mistake shows a misunderstanding of the Cavalier Creed, which ought to have been expounded more clearly. The fact is, despite the general atmosphere of cheerfulness in court and city, "in good king Charles's merry days, when loyalty had no harm in't," we fear that we have too often indulged, like Macbeth's witches, "in riddles and affairs of death"—and thus have shown comparatively little of the contented spirit of our favourites, contrasted with the grimness of the sanctimonious Puritans, who to this day have left their hoof-marks on every green-sward, and on many a countenance. Readers must turn to our *Roxburghe Ballads* and *Bagford Ballads* (many a bulky volume), with their Notes and Introductions, to see the livelier conviviality of Stuart days. The books are not easily attainable (except by payment of the moderate annual subscription to the Ballad Society, through our worthy Printers, Messrs. Austin, of Hertford). But they contain a world of heretofore unreprinted and genuine ditties, with their pictorial embellishments, that carry us back to an interesting period of history, and clothe the dry bones anew with flesh and suitable raiment. The earlier ballads exemplify the truth that life was worth living two centuries ago. Then, as now, it depended on the Liver.

Decidedly we feel no inclination towards Pessimism. Such misbelief is destructive to all real progress or happiness. Let this be taken as a proclamation of our Cavalier Creed (written 4, xii. '82) :—

Early to Rest.

" Ah me ! if our heart should grow chilly,
  With the sad flight of years after youth,
Seeking stains in the purest white lily,
  Or mocking Love's fervour and truth !
It seems better to slip off betimes, dear,
  Ere the best of the feast is gone by,
Than to deal out dull cynical rhymes, dear :
  (Though we feel in no hurry to die).
Lads and Lasses, be happy, leave wise saws untold,
  Take your joy in the present, your own Age of Gold ;
Whom the Gods love are cheerful, and never grow old.
  Mavourneen ! mavourneen ! so no one need scold."

Students of life, with Cavalier instincts and no Puritanical dyspepsia, take an optimistic view of all around them, leaving persons who are already discontented to brood over Schopenhauer for enlivenment of their dormant faculties. Students of literature, who associate with their own class only, are apt to take jaundiced views, while perhaps literary jealousies and quarrels help to sadden them more than the inevitable troubles of town life. Living or dead they are the prey of vampires, like our departed friend Clarens, or Mortimer Collins :—

Ambition Gratified.

Said Clarens—" Thus far my hopes extend,
That many an Editor call me friend ;
From my *Opus Magnum* every day
May they quote my sayings, grave or gay."

Poor Clarens might starve, but his wish came true :
In the *Scintillator* his light we view :
His fancies have not into darkness flown,
For the Editors flash them out—as their own.

Page 147.—"*Brocade and 'Hwang.*" If there be any unfortunate being who does not know Austin Dobson's "Ballad of Beau Brocade," the Highwayman who was captured by Dolly the Chambermaid (*Old World Idylls*), or Andrew Lang's delightful "*XXII Ballades in Blue China*," one of which tells of what happened "in the reign of the Emperor Hwang," let him get the books immediately, and enjoy a treat at his own expense. But let him avoid Gosse-lings, and bury Saints.

Page 148.—*A Leap-Year Birthday Ode* was written, and privately-printed (a few copies, one for each guest at the Bisextile festival) in honour of Miss Jane Hill, daughter of the late Alexander Hill, printseller and publisher, of Edinburgh. Her uncle, D. O. Hill, the celebrated landscape-painter, married Sir Noël Paton's sister, Amelia, the highly accomplished sculptor of the colossal statue of David Livingstone. The final stanza was unconsciously prophetic of the maiden's self-devotion in after-years to the cloister, in France.

Page 152.—*My Friend the Actress.* Only a few months intervened between her marriage with Arthur Boyd Kinnear, and the stilling of her warm heart in death. The only surviving child of an English physician, whose memory she revered, she was an early friend of Ada, Countess of Lovelace (Byron's "Ada, sole daughter of my home and heart," who in girlhood had been shamefully kept in ignorance of his best poetry by his vindictive widow, Lady Byron). Her name of Frankland, at the Theatre Royal, Edinburgh (where she was 'leading lady,' and a great favourite), was merely a professional disguise, and not her true surname. Her noble nature deserves a more solemn *In Memoriam* than this impromptu tribute to her sweetness, courage, and virtue, written before the shadow fell across her path. Yet was Death really a shadow, or a ray of brighter light?

P. 156.—*Richard of Rochester*; p. 175, "*Under the Molash Yews.*" Well-known to Canterbury pilgrims before Chaucer's day, and since, as a halting-place on their way towards the over-rated shrine of Thomas à Becket, was that quiet nook of Kent, holding the ancient Priory and churchyard of Molash. Six yew-trees, of magnificent girth and foliage, encircle the church (undesecrated by ruinous 'Restoration'). Sombre and beautiful, the growth of a thousand years, they guard the mouldering dust of a simple honest race, the industrious labouring poor, who have dwelt there contentedly, within sight of the cathedral city, nine miles distant. Formerly there was a seventh yew-tree, standing on the south side, in front of the vaulted church-porch, and near it a Lych-gate ; but some bygone Vicars of Chilham enriched themselves by carting away the timber, and plundering Molash belfry of its fine peal of bells, mentioned in early chronicles. The last but one of these bells was sold in 1793 on pretence of payment for "repairs," when the summit was removed from the crumbling square tower. An excuse was easily found for Chilham robbing Molash. Even the rich chasubles, "the vestement of blue velvet," the Dalmatics and albs belonging to Molash vestiarium, (*vel* Molesse, A.D. 1305), as enumerated in the reign of Edward VI., were stolen later, and removed to Chilham. (See p. 192.)

Tradition is silent regarding the motives that induced Richard of Rochester to select this humble parish for his final residence. After his busy and adventurous life (a fragment of his writings is copied in *Collectanea Cantiana*, Addit. MS. 24,240, fol. 33 *verso* and 34), his intercourse with bravest men and fairest damosels, he may have learnt to prize the sweet seclusion of such a Kentish Priory, with wooded valleys near, tempting to solitude, while the breeze blew across the meadows from the North Sea. It was not always a deserted village. The stained-glass of the church-windows preserves escutcheons, shields borne by angels, with armorial blazon of nobility and gentry ; proving that the earlier days of Hamo de Molesse and Stephen de Molesse saw many a goodly company gather to worship within these walls. Some of the stone tracery is unsurpassed in beauty. The ancient font of Kentish Ragstone, the long-hidden piscina, even the "holy-water stoup," which Cromwellian iconoclasts partially shattered, lead us back to the old time. A belief survives that the Prior Richard, 'of Rochester,' when little past middle-age, was found dead inside the still-uninjured 'Priest's-chamber' in the North wall (the only residence of the holy man who came to hear confession, and bestow spiritual Absolution on the penitents) ; when he used to gaze through the arched casement towards the pole-star. He lies buried beneath the very tree to which his weary eyes were turned in death. No stone marks the spot, but it is not difficult to recognize. A crowd of crazy fanatics, from Bosenden Wood and Chartham Hatch, defaced the brass memorial tablet in the chancel floor, leaving little decipherable beyond the words,

Hic jacet Ricard. Roffen.

[*Inventories of Parish Church Goods in Kent*, A.D. 1552.]

"MOLYSII, xxviii November   Ed[uard]. VI.

Reygnold Herrys & John Kennay, churchwardens.
Andrew Amye, Thomas Gottbye, John Wanston, parishoners.

Imprimis a chalys off sylver with a paten parcell gylt wayeng
ix ouncys iij quarters, Item a coope & a vestement of blew
velvett, a vestment of whyte damaske.
Item iij alter cloths, Item a pyxe of latyn, Item in the Stepule iij bells,
Item a hand bell.
Item a pyx of latten.
Item caret a whyt coope off damaske stollene, Item v bad chesables & a
bad coope stollen, Item a water pott off latyn, Item a bason & an
ewer of pewter, Item iij alter clothes, Item iij candyllstycks of
latyn and an other lytell bell."—*Archæologia Cantiana*, x. p. 284.

P. 158.—*Grandfather.* A few instances have been recorded of still
greater longevity among cats (see *Notes and Queries*, 5th series, III.
pp. 104, 194), our favourites of the *Purr sang* and Mewses darlings.
'Grandfather,' Patriarch of Felinæ, lived and died contentedly in the
happy service of Mrs. McLaren, of Ivy Lodge, Trinity, near Edinburgh.
In his last days his faithful companion Pussy brought to him captured
mice and birds, as though to tempt a kitten. "Trap," memorialized in
the succeeding page, had belonged to Mrs. De Vaynes, of Cliftonville,
Margate. "Belle" *alias* Puppy, a youthful companion of Trap, showed
her gratitude for his protecting care, after following his corpse to the
grave under the trees at Updown, by frequently trotting off alone to
visit the spot, and by lying there peacefully for an hour before returning
to her home at Cliftonville. Of later years her heart has accepted
another friend 'Boxer,' as the sex generally does. (When Ariadne
was deserted by Theseus at Naxos, she took to Bacchus; but perhaps
this is only an allegory to hint that she consoled herself with d-i-k-ng.
Can this be true?)

Pages 160 to 173.—The four designs representing the seasons are
reduced copies of original woodcuts that adorned sundry broadside
ballads, preserved at the Bodleian and British Museum Libraries.
They had earlier belonged to some untraced foreign book, *temp. Car.* II.

Possibly the tenth section of the poem (displaced from this earliest print of "A Year's Messages") may still find a reader, if introduced here. Like other seven sections, it was written on Dec. 27, 1883; the earlier sections on Dec. 6 (except Autumn, written on August 11, 1868).

X.—OCTOBER. (SPIRITUAL BROTHERHOOD.)

Companionship in all best thoughts or aims
　　With those most fit for us, in meetings rare,
We hold amid our dull world's Isthmian games:
　　True holidays, and breathe a purer air.

With touch of hand, with kindling glance of eye,
　　Our souls' Masonic mystery's interchanged;
Firm grip, sure word and sign, that passers-by
　　Could never reach, while alien laws estranged.

Thus in the Temple-service, high, austere,
　　Fit ministrants are found, long held apart;
Yet meeting when the East-born light shines clear,
　　With stainless hand and with undaunted heart.

Fade the distinctions, born from creed or race,
　　And only native worth with worth can meet:
So in the last great Temple, face to face,
　　Earth's loftiest guides shall gather all complete.

In its recognition of unsectarian catholicity, as the true bond of spiritual union, our lines may not appear orthodox in Parsondom or in Little Bethel; but perhaps they are not the less true on that account. The whole poem, if a poem it can be called, was inscribed to H.M.W., widow of the Rev. A. J. Woodhouse, the noblest and best clergyman whom the author ever knew and loved; that Alfred Joseph Woodhouse, Vicar of Ide-Hill, whom the excellent late Archbishop of Canterbury had in 1876 nominated Bishop of Western Australia (Perth), and with whom, as his chaplain, J.W.E. had unhesitatingly consented to quit England for ever. *Diis aliter visum*, or these "Cavalier Lyrics" would never have been written.

Page 175.—"Under the Molash Yews." Compare the *Note* on p. 190. Molash is now officially misnamed 'Moldash.'

Page 144.—"*Tomes of Ballad lore.*" Here is our own tribute to the earlier ballad-seeker, John Bagford (compare *note* on p. 187).

John Bagford, the Ballad Collector.

(To a well-known Cavalier Tune: 'Which no body can deny.')

" Who saved our street-ballads, two centuries old,
    So rare they are worth their weight twelve times in gold?
    Twelve times ! nay, Collectors would give fifty fold !
        Which no body can deny."
It was famous **John Bagford**, who gather'd the store ;
Deep was he in bibliographical lore ;
His 'Titles' to gain, he wreck'd volumes galore ;
        Which no body can deny.

" Like other Collectors, he did not well look
    To the workmen employ'd in re-binding each book ;
    When heaven sends Broadsides, the fiend sends a cook :
        Which no body can deny.
" Hence it happens, alas ! in his volumes appears
Not alone paste-brush labours, but sad work from shears :
For Book-binders, Midas-like, boast of long ears :
        Which none of them can deny."

We took without grumbling, or swearing too hard,
The *membra disjecta* of each shatter'd bard ;
When reprinting with care, for our nation's regard,
        Which no body can deny.
We found in his ballads, once sold for odd pence,
Much humour, some fancy, and shrewd common-sense :
(Still surviving in England two hundred years thence,)
        Which no body can deny.

They show the world then held two fools for each rogue ;
With bould Oirish Souldiers, half blarney, half brogue :
'Thrue Prothestant Zeal' (most destructive) in vogue,
        Which no body can deny.
They show there were Lawyers, who plunder'd the poor ;
And Misers, who drove them unhelp'd from the door ;
And Light-skirts, as fickle as still can allure :
        Which no body can deny.

They show how we swagger'd, on winning a fight ;
Proving all foes were wrong, while ourselves were quite right :
Folks blacken'd the White-flag, the Orange bleach'd white :
Who ever can this deny ?
But they show, to fit readers, how valour and truth,
With the pure love that blossoms in Beauty and Youth,
Kept their world quite as wholesome as ours, in good sooth :
Which no body can deny.

Readers, haste to the banquet, that Bagford provides !
Though Pedants may sneer, and the Prudish Prig chides ;
Satirical whipcord should tickle their hides,
Which no body can deny.
If in John Bagford's own lot, all here now averr'd
Be not fully borne out, to the uttermost word—
Search the (' *Roxburghe* ') store he to Harley transferr'd :
Then no body can deny.

Ballade, on the Impossible She.

There are stories afloat of a ghost,
  There are stories one cannot believe ;
For, betwixt you and me and the post,
  Some folk seem only born to deceive,
  While around us such lie-lies they weave,
That with horror they make our flesh crawl :
  But they say that, " One Daughter of Eve
Never reads through his ' Lyrics ' at all !"

For my part, I can silence a host
  Of declaimers, whose bellowings ' deave' ;
Noisy praters, who'd fain rule the roast :
  Words cling tightly, like chaff to greased sieve,
  Could we their waste hours retrieve !
Life is short, since they chatter and bawl,
  Saying, " She (to whom love still must cleave)
Never reads through his ' Lyrics ' at all !!"

Are they human, or ghouls, who thus boast ?
  They are fiends, who can murder and thieve ;
I might ask, " Wilt thou swear that thou know'st ?"
  Let one doubt linger still for reprieve,
  It seems hard ev'ry hope to bereave :
Tempts to knock one's own head 'gainst the wall,
  Since these words the dazed mind will not leave :
" Never reads through his Lyrics at all !!!"

L'Envoi.

Fatal Three, who spin, measure, abbrieve
  Our poor thread (whom men Destinies call),
Is aught worse than this stone to up-heave,
  " Never reads through his Lyrics at all ?"

The End.

Table of first Lines.

STEPHEN AUSTIN AND SONS, PRINTERS, HERTFORD.

www.ingramcontent.com/pod-product-compliance
Lightning Source LLC
Chambersburg PA
CBHW020107030726
47498CB00006B/1996